A TRAITOR AMONG THE BOYS

■ ■ ■ ■ ■ ■

A TRAITOR AMONG THE BOYS

■

Phyllis Reynolds Naylor

A DELL YEARLING BOOK

To Katie Billingsley

35 Years of Exceptional Reading

Dell Yearling Books
Established 1966

Published by
Dell Yearling
an imprint of
Random House Children's Books
a division of Random House, Inc.
1540 Broadway
New York, New York 10036

Visit us on the Web! www.randomhouse.com/kids

Educators and librarians, for a variety of teaching tools, visit us at www.randomhouse.com/teachers

ISBN: 0-440-41386-9

Reprinted by arrangement with Delacorte Press

Printed in the United States of America

January 2001

10 9 8 7 6 5 4 3

OPM

Contents

■ ■ ■ ■ ■ ■

One

■

New Year's Resolution

"**O**kay, then, it's decided. The girls can stay," Jake said, looking around the breakfast table, where six different boxes of cereal were scattered. "But *only,*" he added, his mouth full of Frosted Flakes, "if they play by our rules."

As though they had anything to do with the Malloys staying in or leaving West Virginia.

The first week of January had passed, and the boys had still not made their New Year's resolutions. Mrs. Hatford had given an order: they were not to leave the kitchen until each had decided how he would improve as a human being in the 365 days ahead. Jake, Josh, Wally, and Peter decided it would be easier to come up with one joint resolution they could all do together: they would let the Malloy girls stay in the house across the river where their best friends, the Bensons—all boys—used to live.

1

Mrs. Hatford came into the kitchen just then to get the watering can for her fern.

"Well?" she said. "Do I hear four good resolutions in the making?"

"No, but we have one really good one that we'll all do together," said Josh, Jake's eleven-year-old twin.

Their mother looked cautiously about the table. "Okay, I'm listening."

Wally Hatford, age nine, who was sitting beside seven-year-old Peter, the youngest, stuffed another bite of toast into his mouth so that he wouldn't be the one to answer, because he could almost predict what his mom was going to say.

"We've decided," said Jake, "that we'll let the Malloys live in Buckman, if they want to, after their year is up."

Mrs. Hatford slowly removed her glasses and her eyes traveled from Jake to Josh to Wally to Peter.

"*Let* them?" she asked in disbelief. "Are they renting their house from *you*?"

"What we mean," said Josh, "is that we won't make things hard for them anymore."

Mrs. Hatford focused on Wally next. "Meaning . . . ?" she asked. It *always* happened this way: Wally got the hard questions.

"Meaning that we won't dump dead fish and birds on their side of the river to make them think it's polluted," Wally said miserably.

Peter nodded vigorously. "Or dead squirrels," he said. "Don't forget the squirrels."

Their mother put one hand on the back of a chair

to steady herself, and finally came around and sat down on its seat. Hard.

"Do you boys mean to sit here and tell me that you actually tried to drive the Malloys out of Buckman? That you tried to get them to move back to Ohio?"

Wally thought it over. *Was this a trick question?* "Yep," he said.

"Why?"

"Because we wanted the Bensons to come back," Josh told her. "They were the best friends we ever had."

"And you thought—you thought—" Mrs. Hatford began, "that if you drove the Malloys away, the Bensons would return?"

"Something like that," said Jake, looking a little chagrined. "We thought it might help, anyway."

"Are you completely, positively out of your minds?" Mrs. Hatford yelled. "Have you lost every ounce of common sense you were born with? Did it ever occur to you that the decision will be based on whether the Bensons like it well enough to stay in Georgia, and not on what is happening up here to their house?"

"Well, if they lost their renters, we thought they'd at least consider coming back," said Josh.

Mrs. Hatford slumped in the chair and closed her eyes for a moment.

"All right," she said weakly. "Let's hear it. What else did you do?"

The boys leaned their elbows on the table and thought about it—Jake and Josh in their sweatpants and T-shirts, Wally in his racing-car pj's, and Peter in his Bambi pajamas with a tail on the seat of the pants.

"We howled outside their house once when the girls were alone," Wally ventured, probably the least offensive thing they had done.

"We locked Caroline in the toolshed," said Peter.

Mrs. Hatford gasped.

"But we let her out when we thought she was getting rabid," Wally said quickly.

Their mother could only stare.

"We messed up the pumpkin chiffon pie their mother sent over and spied on Beth's bedroom and got them lost in the woods," said Jake.

Mrs. Hatford buried her face in her hands. "What else?" she asked, her voice high and tight.

Wally felt miserable seeing his mom that way. The four brothers exchanged anxious looks.

"That's about it," said Wally.

Mrs. Hatford dropped her hands again. "I want a *full* confession!" she demanded. "Don't leave out a single thing."

The boys sighed in unison and tried to think some more.

"We took a worm when they invited us over at Thanksgiving and put it on Caroline's plate," said Jake.

"And we *were* going to dump a can of worms on them one night in the cemetery, but they never showed up," Josh remembered.

"And how about the night we trapped Caroline in the cellar of Oldakers' Bookstore and she couldn't get

4

out?" said Wally, smiling a little as he remembered, then just as suddenly wiping the smile off his face.

Slowly Mrs. Hatford stood up. "I am surprised, frankly, that the Malloys *are* still here. I am surprised that Jean and George are speaking to us at all!"

"Well, it's not as though they never did anything to *us*!" said Jake. "They've done plenty!"

"And all of it deserved, I imagine," Mrs. Hatford said, just as her husband wandered into the kitchen for his second cup of coffee.

He looked curiously about him. "What did I miss?" he asked.

"Don't ask," said Mrs. Hatford. "Don't ask."

Wally didn't know if this meant the conversation was over and he could make his escape or not. He slowly inched his chair away from the table.

"Stay right where you are!" Mrs. Hatford said. Wally froze.

It was Mr. Hatford who made his escape. He poured his coffee and immediately left the room, as though he couldn't get away fast enough.

Jake and Josh didn't move, because their mother was looking right at them.

"Now get this," she said. "You are not only going to *let* the Malloys stay in Buckman if they like, you are going to be *nice* to those girls. You are going to be helpful, polite, friendly, and whatever else I can think of for as long as they live in our town."

"Forever?" gasped Wally. He could see himself being helpful, polite, and friendly for an afternoon, maybe—a day, perhaps. Maybe even a whole week. But *forever*?

"Forever," said Mrs. Hatford. "Beginning now. I don't want to hear of one unkind word, one scowl, one argument. . . . I want you to treat those girls as though they were your sisters."

Wally instantly felt better. If the Hatfords had sisters, he was sure they wouldn't always get along. They wouldn't always be polite to each other. Jake and Josh must have been thinking the same thing, because they didn't look quite so uncomfortable now either.

"Like *sisters*!" Mrs. Hatford repeated.

"Like sisters," Jake promised.

"I think I'll go lie down," Mrs. Hatford said. "I've only been up an hour, and I'm ready to go back to bed."

The boys went into the living room and spread out in front of the fireplace with the morning comics. Their father was reading the sports section at the dining room table, so the boys had the living room to themselves. Jake was actually grinning.

"Since we've never had sisters . . . ," he began softly.

". . . And we don't know *how* we would treat them if we did . . . ," added Josh.

". . . I figure we can do about whatever we like," finished Jake. "We'd probably treat sisters the same way we treat each other, and *we* don't always get along. We fight and argue and play tricks all the time."

"Right!" said Wally. "We just won't lock anyone in the toolshed anymore."

"Or spy in their bedroom windows," said Josh. "Especially Beth's."

"If they ever give us a pumpkin pie again, we won't tear it apart looking for dog doo," said Wally.

Peter said nothing, but he looked happy. He looked, in fact, like a second-grade boy who liked the Malloy girls and was glad things were going to be better between their two families. He looked like a boy who, having just finished breakfast, was already thinking of lunch, and remembering the cookies he occasionally got, baked by Eddie, Beth, and Caroline Malloy.

And so, while his brothers were reading the comics, Peter put on his clothes, pulled on his boots, got his coat from the closet, and set out over the swinging bridge to the house on the other side of the river.

■ ■ ■ ■ ■ ■ ■ ■ ■ ■ ■

Two

■

Early-Morning Visitor

"Here's something that might interest you, girls," said Mrs. Malloy, glancing at the morning paper as she buttered her toast. "The town of Buckman will be two hundred years old on January twenty-first."

"That doesn't particularly interest me," said Eddie, the oldest, who was eleven. "If *I* was going to be two hundred years old on the twenty-first, I'd be interested. I'd expect the biggest birthday party I'd ever had." Eddie was wearing a pair of pajamas that looked like a baseball uniform because it *was* a baseball uniform. She'd worn it back in Ohio when she was on the girls' softball team, and it was about the most comfortable garment she'd ever had on.

"It doesn't interest me at all!" said Beth, who was ten. She was baking still another batch of cookies, and the kitchen smelled like cinnamon. Beth had begun baking cookies to sell before Christmas, and now, it seemed, she couldn't stop. Every few days she thought up new recipes, and cookie sheets covered the stove, the countertops, even the top of the microwave.

Their mother went on reading, directing her comments to Caroline, who was eight. Caroline was precocious, however, so she was a year ahead in school and in the very same fourth-grade class as Wally Hatford.

"It *says*," Mrs. Malloy continued, "that in addition to a concert by the high-school band and speeches by county officials, the Buckman Community Players are going to perform a little play about the founding of the town. Last week somebody came across an old story about Buckman at the library, and the Players want to use it as part of the celebration. Tryouts are tomorrow. Because they have only two weeks to rehearse, they're looking for actors and actresses who will be available for practice several nights a week."

Caroline's spoon clattered down into her bowl, making a splash of milk and cornflakes.

"Can *anyone* try out?" she asked.

"That's what it says. They're looking for a tall man to play the sheriff, a short man to play the mayor, five women, two boys, and three girls."

"I'll be one of the girls!" cried Caroline, deliriously happy. She leaped from her chair and went dancing about the room. "I don't care what kind of girls they are, I want to be in the play! Does it say how old they have to be, Mother?"

Mrs. Malloy scanned the paper again and took a bite of toast. "No. Just 'three girls.' That's all it says."

"Maybe one will be horribly, horribly wicked!" Caroline said in delight. Her great ambition in life was to be an actress on Broadway, and she knew that starting out small was better than not starting out at all. This would be better than a class play at school. This was for the whole town to enjoy, and some of the actors were grown-ups. It would be her very first role in a grown-up play, if only she could get a part.

"Maybe one of the girls will be a singer or dancer," she went on. "Maybe she'll be such a beautiful girl that everybody hates her, or maybe she's always rescuing little lost animals, and—"

"Or maybe she's sickly and gets to die onstage," said Beth, who had her nose stuck in a cookbook. "Caroline, muffle it, please."

"I'm going to try out! I've got to try out! Oh, Beth, why don't you and Eddie try out too! Maybe the three of us will get the parts!" Caroline continued excitedly.

"No way!" said Eddie. "I'd rather have all my teeth pulled than stand up onstage and act stupid."

"Beth?" Caroline pleaded. "Oh, please! We've never been in a play together, ever!"

"I don't know, I'd have to read the script first. If it's just a bunch of people talking about how wonderful Buckman is, then no. It has to have character and plot and suspense!"

"But *maybe* you'll do it?" Caroline said. "Please? *Please?*"

"I'll think about it," Beth told her, and at that exact moment the doorbell rang.

Caroline, who was dressed in a pink robe with rosebuds on it, got up immediately to answer. She thought she looked like a beautiful princess in the robe, and the more people who saw her, the better.

But Beth, who had started baking that morning in a pair of pajamas that looked like a tiger's skin, yelled, "Don't let anyone in!" The tops and bottoms were yellow with black stripes and were the ugliest pajamas she had ever seen. They even had footpads that looked like claws. The only reason she was wearing them at all was that her grandmother had given them to her for Christmas, and Mrs. Malloy insisted that Beth wear them at least once before she wrote a thank-you note.

Caroline went out in the hall and opened the front door. There stood Peter Hatford smiling up at her, another tooth missing.

"It's only Peter," Caroline called over her shoulder to Beth. Then she opened the door wide and said, "Hi, Peter. Come on in."

"Hello, Peter," Mrs. Malloy called from the living room, where she had taken her toast and coffee. "How are you?"

"I'm hungry!" Peter said, grinning, and headed straight for the kitchen, where the cookies were kept.

Mr. Malloy, who was coach of the football team at the college, watched the young boy disappearing down the hall toward the kitchen. "Did you have a nice Christmas?" he called after him.

"Yeah, it was great!" Peter said. "Especially all the cookies and stuff!"

Out in the kitchen, he sat right down at the table.

"Hi, Peter," said Beth. "Bet I know what you want."

"Yeah! Chocolate, if you have them," said Peter.

"You know what I've decided, Peter?" Beth told

him. "I want to be a pastry chef. Someday I'm going to enter the Pillsbury Bake-Off and win a million dollars. If I do, I'll start my own bakery. This morning I'm making chocolate surprise cookies, with Hershey's Kisses inside."

"Wow!" said Peter.

Eddie got herself some more orange juice from the refrigerator and studied Peter skeptically. "You guys were sure making a lot of noise at your place on New Year's Eve," she said. "Sounded like you were banging together every pot and pan in your house. And who was playing that awful trumpet?"

"That was Jake!" Peter grinned. "We each got to blow it once, though. We brought in the new year, right?"

"Right. You brought it in with a bang," Eddie told him.

Beth put some cookies in front of Peter and got a glass for his milk.

"Guess what *I'm* going to do," said Caroline. "I'm going to start out the new year by being in a play. I'm going to try out for it, anyway."

"We're going to do something too!" Peter told her. "Jake and Josh and Wally and me. We're going to do a revolution!"

"A revolution?" asked Eddie.

"Yeah. Mom said we each had to make a revolution, so we all made one together."

"You mean *resolution*?" asked Beth.

Peter stuffed half a cookie in his mouth and happily swung his legs beneath the table. "Yeah," he said.

"Your mom said you each had to make a New Year's resolution, but you all made one together?"

"Yep. We're all going to do it," said Peter.

"What's the resolution?" asked Eddie.

Peter thought for a moment. "Is it supposed to be a secret?" he asked.

Eddie, Beth, and Caroline exchanged glances.

"Why, I don't think so, do you, Beth?" asked Eddie. "Is there a rule that you have to keep a New Year's resolution secret?"

"I never heard that before," said Beth.

"Me either," said Caroline. "So what was it, Peter? What are you going to do?"

"Be nice to you," said Peter.

Caroline and her sisters stared.

"Be nice to *us*?" Beth choked.

He nodded. "Yep!" He popped the rest of the cookie in his mouth, and little crumbs fell from his lips onto the table. "We said we were going to let you stay in Buckman if you wanted, but Mom said we have to be nice and polite and friendly *forever*."

Slowly, Eddie in her baseball uniform, Beth in her tiger pj's, and Caroline in her rosebud robe turned to grin at each other and then at Peter. The three of them sat down and crowded around him.

"What exactly will your resolution mean?" asked Eddie. "What does it mean you will or won't do?"

"Well," said Peter, "we can't ever drop dead squirrels on your side of the river again, and we can't lock Caroline in the toolshed, and if you ever give us another pie, we can't mess it up looking for dog doo."

Caroline tried not to laugh.

"But what are you going to do *for* us?" asked Eddie. "What are you going to do that's nice and polite and friendly?"

Peter bit into another cookie and chewed. Finally he took a swallow of milk, then shrugged.

"Treat you like sisters," he said.

Three

■

A Little Conversation

Wally woke up the next morning to cold. The air was cold, the pillow was cold, his nose—the only thing sticking out of the covers—was cold. But the space under the blankets was toasty warm, and Wally did not want to get up again ever.

With one finger he pulled the covers down a little so he could peek out. The window was coated with frost. In fact, it made a pattern that looked like the continent of Africa, except that it had a rather large lump where a lump shouldn't be.

Wally loved to study things. He could easily stay under the blankets the rest of the day, he thought, just looking at the frost on the window or the crack in the ceiling or the spiderweb that was strung from—

"Wally, I won't tell you again!" came his mother's voice from the doorway. "Get up and get dressed. There's oatmeal on the stove if you want it."

Wally closed his eyes, counted to twenty, then

threw off the covers and, like a soldier going into battle, grabbed his clothes and headed for the warmth of the bathroom. Josh was already in there, however, taking a shower.

"Arrrggghhh!" howled Wally.

"For goodness' sake, he'll be out in a few minutes," said Mrs. Hatford. "For once in my life, I'd like to see four boys get themselves off in the morning without any uproar whatsoever."

Mornings in the Hatford household were always hectic because Mr. Hatford was a mail carrier who had to be at work by eight-thirty, the boys had to be at school by nine, and Mrs. Hatford had to be at her job at the hardware store by nine-thirty. So the family showered in shifts, and the part of the morning that Mrs. Hatford liked best, she said, was when everyone else was gone and she could enjoy a cup of coffee in peace.

"Well, maybe by now things will have settled down some at the P.O.," Mr. Hatford said as he put his blue sweater on over his blue shirt, his blue jacket over his blue sweater. He put on a blue cap with blue earmuffs, and finally, with a "Have a good day, Ellen," and then, "You too, guys," he went out the door.

At last the boys were bundled up, ready to go. Teeth were brushed, homework collected, lunches packed, and they set off out the door.

"Let's get to school before we run into the girls," Jake said. "I don't feel like being nice to anyone this morning."

"We *have* to be nice," said Peter. "Mom *said*."

"Just come on," Jake grumbled, but no sooner had they got to the end of the driveway than they saw the three Malloy girls coming over the swinging bridge that crossed the Buckman River.

The river came into town from one direction, circled around the end of Island Avenue, and flowed back out again on the other side. A road bridge at the end of Island Avenue connected the few houses there to the business district only two blocks away, but the narrow swinging footbridge furnished a shortcut over to College Avenue, where the Hatfords lived.

The girls were headed for school.

"Hi," said Josh, trying his best to be friendly, as he'd promised. He and his twin brother were as different as salt and pepper, but they really got along well. Jake was usually the ringleader of the bunch, full of energy and ideas. Josh had ideas too, but he liked to draw almost more than he liked eating or sleeping. He could draw pictures of anything, but he especially liked drawing airplanes, aliens, race cars, and horses.

"Hi," said Beth, smiling back.

No one frowned at anybody, and Peter looked from one to another, happy that finally, it seemed, his brothers, whom he loved, and the Malloy girls, whom he liked very much, appeared as though they might possibly get along.

When they had gone another half block and nobody had said anything particularly mean, Peter chirped, "Isn't it nice that we're all being friendly?"

"Shut up, Peter," muttered Jake.

But Caroline said, "Well, I think January's going to be wonderful, because guess what? Buckman is celebrating its two hundredth anniversary. The Buckman Community Players are putting on a play, and *I'm* going to be in it."

"You?" said Wally. "What are you going to be? The dog?"

As soon as the words were out of his mouth, he realized that this did not sound friendly or nice at all, so he added quickly, "I mean, is this a play about people or animals?" He tried to make it sound as polite as possible.

"People, of course!" said Caroline. "About the founding of the town of Buckman."

"Whoop-de-doo! Now, that ought to be a real sell-out!" said Jake.

"They're looking for two boys," Caroline added. "Why don't some of you try out for the parts?"

"I'd rather have my fingernails pulled out one by one," said Jake.

Beth studied him. "That's funny. Eddie said she'd rather have her teeth pulled out than get up on a stage."

"I don't want my teeth *or* my fingernails pulled out!" Peter declared warily.

The sky was gray, the air was cold, and the snow that was left on the ground was old and dirty. It seemed to Wally as though the new year could at least bring in some new snow. Why should they have to keep going to the same old school in the same old town in the same old snow that had been around for days?

He didn't know much about how Buckman got started, but he didn't think the two hundredth anniversary could be all that great a celebration. "Wait till June when we have the strawberry festival," he said. "Now, *that's* worth seeing. There's a strawberry parade, a strawberry float, strawberry ice cream, strawberry pie. . . ."

"Is there a strawberry princess?" Caroline wanted to know. "If there is, I'm going to try out for it."

"Ha!" said Wally, and he would have said more, but he remembered he was supposed to be nice to the girls. It was just that Caroline really bugged him sometimes. Whenever there was a part to be played center stage, Caroline wanted to be there, in the spotlight if possible.

The old brick building loomed up ahead, and he tried to prepare himself for Miss Applebaum, who always had a pile of work waiting.

The girls went on ahead; Peter followed, then Josh, then Wally, then—

Wally turned around.

Jake was a few feet behind him, packing a huge ball of dirty snow in his two gloved hands.

And just as Eddie put her feet on the top step and reached out to open the door, Jake drew his arm back and took aim.

"Jake!" Wally warned him.

"Treat them like sisters, remember?" Jake said, and let the snowball fly.

At that exact moment Eddie opened the door and stepped back to let Peter go through. The snowball went flying right through the doorway and into the face of the principal.

Four

■

Big, Big Mistake

Caroline, Beth, and Eddie could only stare.

The big fat snowball positively exploded in Mr. Kelly's face. Clumps of snow skittered down his shirt-front, then onto his shoes.

The principal leaned forward, removed his glasses and shook them, then pulled a handkerchief from his pants pocket and wiped his face.

Out on the sidewalk, the Hatford boys froze like toy soldiers facing the enemy. When Mr. Kelly put his glasses on again, his eyes fell at once on Eddie, who was still holding the door open.

"I'm sorry," said Eddie. "I missed."

Caroline gasped in astonishment.

"You *missed*?" the principal repeated.

"Yes. That snowball was thrown to me and I didn't catch it."

Beth and Caroline looked at each other. Out on the

sidewalk, the Hatford boys' mouths fell open one by one, first Jake's, then his brothers'. *Why* was she covering for Jake?

"You know the rules about snowballs on the playground!" Mr. Kelly thundered.

"Yes, sir, but we were only practicing for the baseball team. We weren't having a snowball fight."

Caroline blinked.

Mr. Kelly stepped to the door and looked out at the Hatford brothers and the other children who were waiting to come in. Then he looked again at Eddie.

"*You* were practicing for the baseball team?"

"Yes, sir. And usually I'm very, *very* good. If *I'd* been the pitcher instead of the catcher, this wouldn't have happened." She gave him her most winsome smile.

But Mr. Kelly still had a big red mark on his forehead. As much as Eddie wanted to make the team, come April, Caroline could not believe she had taken the blame for a snowball meant for her.

"Who were you playing catch with?" Mr. Kelly asked.

"I threw it," said Jake, stepping forward suddenly.

"You will not go down to the gym for morning recess," the principal said. "You will stay in your classroom, and Eddie will write *I will not play catch with snowballs* one hundred times on the blackboard while Jake watches. Jake will wipe it off. Then you will both stay in your classroom for afternoon recess. Jake will write *I will not play catch with snowballs* one hundred times while Eddie watches. Then Eddie will wipe it off. And if I see you throwing snowballs again on the playground, you will both be banned from the team. Is that understood?"

"Yes," said Jake.

"Yes," said Eddie, and Caroline didn't think she had ever seen her sister look happier.

Mr. Kelly went on down the hall. The Hatford boys scattered as soon as they got inside, but Caroline and Beth crowded around Eddie as she stopped by the drinking fountain.

"Are you out of your mind?" asked Beth. "Why did you take half the blame for Jake? He wasn't being nice to us at all! You *know* he tried to hit you with that snowball. So much for his New Year's resolution."

But Eddie's eyes were shining. "Didn't you hear what the principal said? If I throw any more snowballs on school property I'm banned from the team. That means if I *don't* throw any snowballs, I'm *not* banned. I *can* try out! He practically said so."

So that was it, Caroline realized. Eddie's mind was as quick as her pitching arm. She herself would never have been able to think up something so fast.

Eddie grabbed her sisters' arms. "But I'm not through with Jake yet! Wait for me after school at that big oak tree just off the playground. We want to be waiting when the boys go by."

Caroline had two wonderfully exciting things to think about all day—the tryouts for the Buckman Community Players that evening, and what Eddie was going to do to Jake that day after school.

Wally, however, who sat in front of Caroline in

Miss Applebaum's class, seemed completely baffled by what Eddie had done. As the other kids were hanging up their coats, he turned around in his seat and asked, "What got into Eddie?"

Caroline shrugged and looked as innocent as she could manage. "I don't know! I guess she was just feeling . . . well, a little sisterly today, that's all."

When the fourth-graders went out for recess that morning, Caroline went by the sixth-grade classroom, and there was Eddie writing *I will not play catch with snowballs* one hundred times on the blackboard, while Jake, looking as puzzled as Caroline had ever seen him, watched.

When the fourth-graders went out for recess that afternoon, Caroline went by the sixth-grade classroom again, and there was Jake writing *I will not play catch with snowballs* with Eddie watching, and Eddie still had a sly little smile on her face.

Caroline had her books all ready at three o'clock, so as soon as the bell rang, she grabbed her jacket and was the first one out the door.

She was halfway across the playground before anyone else even came out of the building, and was soon joined at the oak tree by Beth and Eddie.

"What's up?" asked Beth.

"You mean, what's *down*," said Eddie, her eyes beginning to glower. "Or, what's *going* to be down. *Jake's* going to be down, that's what." She led her sisters over to a hedge just beyond the school property. "We're going to wait here," she said, "and when the Hatfords come by, we're going to leap on Jake—all three of us. Before Wally and Josh can even think of stopping us, we are going to stuff Jake so full of snow he'll think he's a snowman. Beth, you push snow down his collar; Caroline, you rub snow in his face; and I'm going to cram a snowball right into his mouth. As soon as you're done, run like crazy and I'll meet you at home."

When Eddie got even, she didn't fool around.

Beth looked at her older sister uncertainly. "Isn't this just going to start the war all over again?"

"All over again?" asked Eddie. "It never stopped! If the war was over, how come Jake was trying to plaster me against the school door with a giant snowball?"

"Yeah, but if we try to get even, then *they'll* try to get even, and it will just go on and on."

"Trust me," said Eddie.

So the girls hid behind the hedge, backpacks firmly secured so they could make a quick getaway. When other kids passed, they pretended they were just standing there having a casual conversation, but when they heard the Hatford boys coming down the sidewalk, they flattened themselves against the bushes and prepared to jump.

". . . I *told* you they were nice!" Peter was saying.

"I can't understand it," came Josh's voice. "If Eddie hadn't taken part of the blame, Jake, you would have been toast!"

"I don't know. . . ." Wally's voice now. "I have a feeling they're up to something. Eddie wouldn't do something like that without—"

The boys passed the hedge and the girls leaped.

Eddie tackled Jake's legs.

Beth sat on him.

Caroline grabbed a handful of snow and rubbed it in his face.

It was hard to tell what was happening because the boys were yelling, feet were kicking, arms were flying, and the next thing Caroline knew, Beth and Eddie were running in two different directions. Caroline herself headed for the backyard of the nearest house as fast as her legs would carry her.

Around a tree, under a clothesline, through a gate, over a fence, but the boys were still gaining.

Why were they all after *her*? It had been Eddie's idea, after all. Yet here came the Hatfords, howling like hyenas, and before she knew it she was in the Hatfords' own backyard, backed into a corner next to the house.

■ ■ ■ ■ ■ ■ ■ ■ ■ ■ ■

Five

■

Trapped

Caroline looked more frightened than Wally had ever seen her. She looked like a cat trapped by a pack of wild dogs. She looked, in fact, as if she were about to die. To cry, anyway.

It was Peter, though, who was crying.

"We're supposed to be friendly," he wept, afraid of what they might do to Caroline. "We're supposed to be *nice*."

"Was it friendly of them to stuff snow down my neck?" Jake bellowed.

"But that was probably Eddie's idea, not Caroline's," Josh reminded him.

Jake was confused. Why *did* Eddie take part of the blame for smacking the principal in the kisser with a snowball? And if she was willing to do that, why did she turn on him and practically suffocate him with snow? There was absolutely no understanding girls.

"I think you're crazy, all three of you!" he told Caroline. "I think the Malloys are all a little bit nuts."

"Okay," said Caroline meekly. "Can I go home now?"

"Yeah, Jake, let her go," Wally said, eager to get inside and have a snack. "You know—treat her like a sister."

"Oh, no, she's not going to get off that easy," said Jake. "Bring her in the house."

So Caroline, with Josh on one side of her and Wally on the other, was escorted up the back steps. She waited while Jake opened the door with the house key.

"Sit down on a chair," Jake commanded, throwing his backpack on the table.

Caroline sat.

"Whose idea was it to ambush us?" asked Jake.

"Whose idea was it to throw that snowball at Eddie?" Caroline retorted.

"Mine, but I didn't hit her. If I'd hit her, I could see why she'd want to fight, but I missed her!" Jake said.

Caroline shrugged. "I guess you'll have to ask Eddie," she said. "Can I go now?"

"No, you can't go! Eddie has to learn she can't go around tackling people!" Jake yelled.

The phone began to ring.

"Mom!" said Wally.

Their mother always called from the hardware store to see if everything was all right if the boys didn't call her the minute they got in the door. She had to be sure a murderer hadn't followed them home.

27

"Don't answer!" said Jake. "Caroline will start yelling and Mom will know she's here."

Riiiing went the phone again.

"Tie a dish towel around her mouth," Jake instructed Wally.

"Make it a clean one," Caroline murmured.

Wally sighed. This always happened. Jake thought up some crackbrained scheme, and it was Wally who had to carry it out. If he tried to tie a dish towel around Caroline Malloy's mouth, she'd probably bite him.

"Hurry up!" Jake yelled, one hand on the phone. "If we don't answer in five rings, she'll probably call the police!"

Wally grabbed a dish towel and wrapped it around Caroline's face while Josh bound her arms to the chair with his jacket. Caroline sat as still as a frog on a log.

Jake lifted the receiver. "Hello?" he said. "Oh, hi, Mom. We just got in. . . . Yeah, everything's okay. . . ." He looked at Caroline. Caroline didn't blink. He hoped she was still breathing. "Yeah?" he said. "Yeah . . . okay. Bye." And he hung up.

Jake turned and faced his brothers. "She said she'll be working late tonight, and if we get hungry we should open a can of chili."

"I'm hungry!" said Peter. "I want a cookie."

Wally unfastened the dish towel from around Caroline's mouth. He was hungry too. He looked in the refrigerator for leftover pizza or something. There was a dish of peas and mushrooms, and half a jar of lima beans.

"Let her go, Jake. Let's get something to eat," Wally said.

"Yeah, let me untie her," said Josh.

Peter lifted the lid of the cookie jar and gave a howl. "They're gone! We ate all the cookies!"

"Will you all shut up while I think?" said Jake. "What would be the right punishment for a girl who rubs snow in your face?"

"Drop ice cubes down her back?" ventured Wally, wishing they could just get it over with and send Caroline on her way.

"We're supposed to treat her like a sister!" Peter insisted. "Make her bake us some cookies."

Jake looked at Peter. Then he looked at Josh and Wally. "Good idea, Peter!" he said. "Bake us some cookies, Caroline."

"All right," she agreed as Josh untied her arms, "but you'd better call my sisters and tell them where I am."

"Oh, no!" said Jake. "I'm not having Beth and Eddie charging over here to rescue you. Bake us some cookies and then you can go. In fact, make it brownies. Make us some brownies."

"Show me where the flour and sugar and stuff are," Caroline said.

They found a recipe on a box of cocoa, and Caroline read off the ingredients. The boys found them for her. Jake turned on the oven and got out a baking pan. Then he made sure that the back door was locked so that she couldn't escape, and—with the key in his pocket—went into the living room with his brothers to watch TV.

"Hey!" said Jake, his feet up on the coffee table. "This is the life! Sitting out here watching TV while our slave bakes up a batch of brownies for us. Not bad!"

"Yeah!" said Peter happily. "I *like* having a sister!"

Out in the kitchen, Caroline began to sing.

The boys switched from one channel to another as the sound of mixing and scraping and stirring came from the other room. The oven door opened, the oven door closed, and there was the noise of spoons and bowls being set in the sink. Very soon the boys began to smell the wonderful chocolate fragrance of brownies.

Caroline came out of the kitchen with her jacket and book bag.

"I have to eat an early dinner because I'm going to try out for the Buckman Community Players," she said. "The brownies should be done at twenty past four. You're supposed to take them out and let them sit for five minutes before you cut them. Can I go?"

Jake went into the kitchen and opened the oven door. There were the brownies, beginning to puff up in the pan.

"Okay," he said. "You can go. But tell Eddie if she ever ambushes us like that again, we'll drag her in here and make her bake us a three-layer cake."

"Yeah!" said Peter. "A *chocolate* cake."

Wally closed his eyes. He couldn't imagine dragging Eddie anywhere. A tiger, maybe, but not Eddie Malloy.

"Okay," said Caroline. "Goodbye. Enjoy the brownies." She went to the front door and was soon heading down the path to the swinging bridge and then across the Buckman River.

The boys went out to the kitchen and sat around the table waiting for the brownies to finish baking. Josh opened four cans of Pepsi and passed them around.

"It might be sort of nice to have sisters," he said.

"Providing they always did what you told them to do," said Jake. "I think maybe they've learned their lesson. I'll bet all this time Eddie and Beth have been out looking for Caroline, and they didn't dare call here."

"What are we going to tell Mom about the brownies?" asked Wally. "We *never* bake brownies. She'll want to know where they came from."

"There's only one answer," said Jake. "We'll have to eat them all—every single one." He grinned.

"And wash the bowl and pan," said Josh.

They watched as the minute hand on the clock reached twenty after four. Jake turned off the oven and Josh took a hot pad and pulled out the pan. He set it on top of the stove.

"Yum!" said Peter.

"If we cut the brownies into sixths one way and eighths the other, that'll make forty-eight brownies, or twelve apiece," said Wally. "We've each got to eat a dozen brownies."

"Poor us!" said Jake.

They let the pan cool for five minutes; then Jake did the cutting and carefully lifted them out with a spatula and placed them on a platter. Each boy picked up a brownie with a napkin and blew on it until it was cool enough to eat. Then, all together, they took a bite and grinned at each other and chewed.

And all together, they spit them out.

"Hey! What's *in* these?" cried Jake.

"They're lumpy!" said Josh.

"They're gross!" cried Wally.

"They're awful!" said Peter in dismay.

Jake got a fork from the drawer and dissected a brownie on the table. It was full of lumps and bumps.

He pulled it apart. It was a brownie filled with leftover peas and mushrooms, and half a jar of lima beans.

Six

■

Tryout

Beth and Eddie were coming down the hill when Caroline crossed the bridge.

"Where *were* you?" Beth cried. "Caroline, we've been looking all over for you! We were afraid you'd fallen in the river. Thank goodness Mom's not home or we'd have to explain it all to her. We didn't know whether to call Dad at the college or not."

"We went back to the school and looked all around," said Eddie. "What happened?"

Next to being onstage, Caroline most loved to tell a story. Her eyes flashed as she faced her sisters.

"I was kidnapped and gagged," she said.

"What?" cried Beth. "By who?" And then she gasped. "The Hatfords?"

"The Hatfords," said Caroline dramatically. "They forced me into their house and tied me up."

"What?" shrieked Beth and Eddie together.

33

Caroline had to explain the whole thing, beginning with the phone call from Mrs. Hatford.

"It's all my fault!" Eddie cried. "If I hadn't tackled Jake, this wouldn't have happened. I just didn't want him to think I was *too* friendly for helping him get out of trouble with the principal."

"What did they do to you, Caroline?" Beth asked worriedly.

"They made me bake brownies," Caroline told them.

Her sisters stared.

"They were hungry, and they said if I'd bake brownies, I could go. So I did."

Beth was amazed. "What *kind* of brownies?"

"I used a recipe on a box of cocoa," Caroline told her. "The boys locked the back door so I couldn't get out, and went in the other room to watch TV."

"So you just baked brownies for them like a dutiful slave!" Eddie said indignantly. "Jake thinks he can lob a snowball at me whenever he pleases, and now the guys will think they can kidnap one of us and make us cook for them!"

"Not quite," said Caroline as they reached the door of their rented house and went inside.

Caroline took off her coat and threw it on a chair. She looked at the clock. It was a quarter past four. "In five minutes the Hatfords will go out in the kitchen and turn off the oven. They'll take out the pan of brownies and set it on the stove to cool. And then . . ." She gave a delighted laugh. An evil laugh. "*Then* . . . they will each pick up a brownie, take a

34

big bite, and spit it out, because I filled them full of peas and mushrooms and lima beans."

Beth and Eddie howled with laughter.

"Oh, it serves them right! Can't you just see their faces?" Eddie shrieked, and they were off again.

Mrs. Malloy came in with a sack of groceries. "What's so funny?" she asked. "What's going on? It sounds like a convention of witches in here. I never heard such cackling and braying."

"A little justice is going on," said Eddie. "A little crime and punishment, that's all." And leaving their mother to wonder, the girls went upstairs, where Caroline put her mind on what she would wear to tryouts for the Buckman Community Players.

She wasn't sure what part she would want to play. If she was to try out for the part of a sweet girl with a gentle voice, she should probably come in her pink-and-white dress with lace on the collar. If she was to play an evil daughter, she should wear her gray dress with the metal buttons; if an adventurous girl, her leopard-print skirt. She decided finally on a bright red dress with black tights so that she would stand out from all the others, and then she went into Beth's room.

"I'm going to tryouts tonight," she said. "How do I look?"

Beth studied her for a moment. "Like a girl who wants to stand out from all the others and make sure she gets a part," she said.

"Beth, *please* come and try out," Caroline pleaded. "It would be so much fun if we were in the play together."

"Oh, I don't know. . . . ," Beth began, but Caroline could tell she was wavering.

"Just come with me, then," Caroline begged. "I don't want to go alone."

So the two girls ate dinner early—it was stew night—and set off for the old movie theater three blocks away, which had been abandoned and then reclaimed by the Buckman Community Players.

■

The play's director was clearly worried as she faced the small group assembled there in the front rows of the old theater.

"I know this isn't Broadway," she said, smiling a little, "but I really hoped more people would show up."

"Well, you've got enough girls," someone observed.

"That's right," the director said brightly. "I need only three girls and I've got . . . five . . . six . . . seven! Even enough for understudies."

No, no, thought Caroline. She could not bear to be an understudy.

"But don't worry," the director continued. "We need a group of townspeople who will be in almost every scene. We can use every one of you."

"Tell us about the play," a man suggested. So the director told the story of how two families—a farmer's and a grocer's—decided to incorporate their little settlement and call it Buckman. But there were lots of problems, because the grocer had two lazy sons, and the farmer, who needed all the hired men he could get, had only daughters, and they were needed in the kitchen.

"What were the daughters like?" Caroline asked.

"They were all very different, from what I can determine," said the director. "The oldest was very beautiful. She actually later married one of the grocer's boys, and they managed, by all accounts, to live quite happily. The youngest daughter was a rather quiet girl, I understand, who was said to be sickly."

Caroline was neither the shortest nor the tallest girl there, and doubted that she would be chosen for either the youngest or the oldest daughter. She would have loved to be the beautiful girl or even the sickly one who just lay about the stage and moaned every now and then.

". . . But the middle daughter absolutely drove her parents crazy," the director continued. "If she wasn't in trouble of one kind, people said, she was in trouble of another kind, and a real mischief-maker."

Caroline frantically waved her hand in the air. "That's the part I'd like to try out for," she said excitedly, and was dismayed to see two other hands shoot up.

"Me too," said another girl.

"And me," said someone else.

"That's wonderful. We won't have any trouble finding daughters, will we? But let's think about the other parts," the director said as a few more people arrived, and she went on with her story of the founding of Buckman. There were just enough men to play the roles of Joseph Buckman, the grocer; Ed Smith, the farmer; the mayor; the sheriff; and the two extra women for the female leads, but no boys at all to play Clyde and Elmer, the grocer's sons.

"All right, we'll try out the girls first so they can leave early. We'll start with the youngest daughter. I'll need the smallest girls for that. Who wants to try out?"

Two girls raised their hands. All they had to do was come onstage, cough a little, and lie down on a couch with a towel over their foreheads. The girl who coughed most convincingly got the part, and the other girl became her understudy plus "girl with cat" among the townspeople.

Caroline was glad she hadn't tried out for the sickly daughter, since she didn't even have any lines to say.

"Okay, middle daughter," the director said.

Now there were *four* girls who wanted the part, and they all went onstage together. One girl, named Tracy Lee, seemed to want the role every bit as much as Caroline, even bumping into her once and standing in front of her every chance she got.

"All right, one at a time, I want you to go offstage, then come on again with a very mischievous look on your face," said the director. "I want you to stand center stage and say to the audience, 'So the grocer wants to call our town Buckman, does he, after his family? Why not call it *Beulah,* after *me?* If he thinks it was a big deal when I turned our chickens loose in his store, wait till he sees what I'm going to do on the Fourth of July!' "

The four girls recited these lines a few times and then, one by one, they came out to center stage and said them to the little audience.

The first girl said her lines in a monotone with no expression whatsoever, Caroline thought.

The second girl forgot her lines and talked so softly when she was prompted that she could hardly be heard at all.

Tracy Lee was next, and Caroline's heart sank, for she was very good. Even Caroline had to admit it. She spoke the lines clearly, with great expression, and when she came to the line "Why not call it *Beulah,* after *me?*" she threw out her arms in a grand gesture, and everyone laughed.

She'll get the part, I know they'll give it to her, Caroline thought in dismay.

Tracy Lee walked over to the side of the stage with a smug smile on her face and managed to step on Caroline's toes.

"All right, let's have the last girl," called the director.

Caroline walked out to center stage, reciting the lines in her head, then took a deep breath. In her most distinct voice, hands on her hips, she said, "So the grocer wants to call our town Buckman, does he, after his family? Why not call it *Beulah,* after *me?*" Here she threw one arm grandly out to one side and placed her other hand over her heart. "If he thinks it was a big deal when I turned our chickens loose in his store, wait till he sees what I'm going to do on the Fourth of July!" And then, with the most mischievous look she could muster, Caroline put one finger to her lips, grinned an evil grin, and with a low "Heh, heh, heh," tiptoed offstage.

The others laughed.

"Well, I think we've found our Beulah," the director said, smiling. "Caroline, you'll be Beulah, and

Tracy Lee, who also did a fine job, will be her understudy, as well as 'girl in lace shawl' among the townspeople. Now, who wants to play the eldest daughter? I really need an older girl for this part."

Tracy Lee glared at Caroline. But Caroline was beside herself with joy. This would be her first performance outside of school. She was headed for Broadway, she was sure of it. Only two girls, however, stood up to play the part of the eldest daughter, and one wasn't even as tall as Caroline. They were not very good actresses, either. All the part really required was to hold hands with the stage manager, who was filling in for the part of Elmer, the grocer's oldest boy, look into his eyes, and say, "With you by my side, Elmer, we can do anything."

The first girl was too embarrassed to hold the stage manager's hands and decided she didn't want to try out after all. The second girl sounded as though she were simply reading her lines.

"You know, I really do need a taller girl for this part," the director said, looking out over the small crowd. Her eye fell on Beth. "What about you, dear? What part are you trying out for?"

"Not anything," said Beth.

"Just for me, would you mind coming up here and saying the lines? I'd like to see how the three daughters might look together onstage," the director said.

Beth got up. Almost *anyone* could say the lines better than the others had done, so she didn't mind. She took the hands of the stage manager and said, "With you by my side, Elmer, we can do almost anything."

"That was excellent! Excellent!" the director said.

"Would you please consider taking the part? We need you. We really do. See? You girls are like stair steps, the perfect heights."

Beth had never thought about being an actress. These days she was totally into baking, but she *had* talked once of being a writer, maybe writing a play. It was a new experience, however, for her to stand up before a crowd and be told that she was good, so she said, "I guess so," and everyone clapped.

The two other girls who had tried out for the eldest daughter were given roles to play among the townspeople, and then the girls were dismissed until the following evening, and Caroline and her sister chattered all the way home.

"You were *wonderful,* Beth!" Caroline kept saying. "We're going to have so much fun!"

"I wonder who they'll get to play the part of Elmer," said Beth. "I hope it's someone cute."

"Like Josh Hatford?" Caroline said, and in the light from the drugstore window, she saw Beth blush just a little.

Aha! said Caroline to herself. *Bingo!* She laughed a silent *heh, heh, heh* and thought, *If they think putting lima beans in brownies was a big deal, wait till they see what I'm going to do next.*

Seven

■

Elmer

Mrs. Hatford stood at the door of the refrigerator.

"I can't understand it!" she said. "I was sure there was a dish of leftover peas and mushrooms in here, and now it's gone. And lima beans! What happened to the lima beans?"

Jake, Josh, and Wally were doing homework on the kitchen table.

"We ate them," Jake said quickly.

Mrs. Hatford turned around and stared.

"You *ate* them? You *hate* lima beans!"

"We were hungry," said Josh. "There weren't any cookies."

Mrs. Hatford closed the refrigerator door and studied the boys in front of her. "There weren't any cookies, so you ate lima beans instead? Do you expect me to believe this? I'm not stupid."

Wally figured he'd better head her off before the whole truth came out. "We took care of the peas and mushrooms too, and then we made brownies. Well, one of us did."

"Will wonders never cease!" Mrs. Hatford declared. "I didn't even know you boys knew how to make brownies."

"Shut up, Peter," Jake murmured.

"I didn't say anything!" Peter said.

"Well, don't!" Jake warned him. And then, to their mother, "There was a recipe on a box of cocoa."

"Then where are they? Could I have one?"

"We ate them," said Wally.

"All except the yucky parts," said Peter, and all the brothers turned and glared at him at once.

Mrs. Hatford sighed. "Oh, well. I think I'll make a casserole for dinner. You boys better move your homework to the dining room table."

The twins picked up their books and headed for the other room. Wally followed with the pencils and pens, and Peter set his glass of pop on the dining room table and sat down at one end.

"Listen, Peter," said Jake. "Don't tell Mom that Caroline was here and that she baked the brownies. Mom would get mad. Just keep it secret and we'll never do it again, okay?"

"You'll be nice to her now?" Peter asked.

"Even polite," Jake promised. "Just don't tell Mom."

"Okay," Peter promised, and the boys breathed a sigh of relief.

■

The next morning when Wally came down to breakfast, he saw the corner of an envelope sticking out from under the front door. He picked it up. Josh's name was on it, so he took it to the kitchen, where the twins were eating cereal, and laid it on the table.

"What's this?" asked Josh.

"I don't know. It was under the door," Wally said.

Josh looked at the envelope. The letters of his name had been cut out of a magazine and pasted to the envelope. All the words on the inside had been cut out of magazines too, until they formed a message:

SOMEBODY **really** likes you.
TO **FIND out** who, **come** to 503
MAIN **street** *tonight* **at** 7:15 and *say*
you *came* **to** see about **ELMER.**

Jake was reading the comics. "What is it?" he asked.

Josh stuffed the paper in his back pocket. "Just something dumb," he said.

Wally started to say something, then stopped. If someone took the time to spell out your name with letters cut out of magazines, it must mean something. And why was Josh blushing?

He didn't say anything, however, and on the way to school, Josh hung back until he was walking beside Wally. Jake and Peter were up ahead. "Hey, Wally, do me a favor, huh?" he murmured. "Come downtown with me tonight. I have to see someone about that note."

"Who?" asked Wally.

"I don't know. That's what I'm trying to find out. It said if I went to a certain address at seven-fifteen,

44

I'd find out. Why don't you come with me? I can't ask Jake. He'd make a big deal out of it."

"Sure," said Wally. Jake and Josh usually did everything together. Neither ever asked Wally to do anything with him alone except stuff that always turned out bad—stuff that Wally would end up getting the blame for.

What Wally was thinking about, however, was what he should say to Caroline about those brownies. As they went up the steps to the school, he decided he would say nothing at all. That would really drive her nuts.

She would *want* to think she'd grossed them out. She would *want* to know they'd spit out the peas and mushrooms. She would *want* to know how they had dissected every single brownie to dig out the lima beans. So he wouldn't tell her any of that.

No sooner had he sat down in his seat than he felt her ruler poking him in the back. He turned around.

"Good morning, Wally!" Caroline chirped, looking angelic. "How did you like the brownies?"

"They were great!" said Wally. "Thanks." He turned back around.

There was silence behind him.

Poke, poke went the ruler again.

Wally turned around.

"You ate them all? Every single one?" asked Caroline.

"Yep," said Wally.

"And . . . and you didn't notice anything?" Caroline asked in dismay.

"Notice what?"

"Well, weren't they sort of lumpy and . . . uh
. . . bumpy?"

Wally shrugged. "I don't know. We ate them so fast
we didn't notice, I guess."

Caroline's face fell.

"Oh," she said.

"Why?" asked Wally.

"Nothing," Caroline said. "I'm glad you enjoyed
them."

■

That evening Jake was doing homework again at
the dining room table when Josh glanced over at
Wally and nodded and they separately left the room.

Outside, pulling on his jacket, Josh said, "It's just
somebody saying she likes me, and I'm curious. It said
if I wanted to find out, I had to go to 503 Main Street
tonight and say I came to see about Elmer."

"Who's Elmer?" asked Wally.

"I don't know. Never heard of him," said Josh.

This was sort of exciting, Wally thought, even
though a girl was probably behind it. Kind of like a
detective story.

"What's at 503 Main?" Wally asked. "Is that
Ethel's Bakery? Oldakers' Books?"

"I don't know," Josh said again.

It wasn't either one. It was the old movie theater.

"You think we should just go in?" Josh asked.

"Maybe we should knock first," Wally suggested.

Josh knocked, softly at first. Then loudly.

There were footsteps inside and a bearded man
opened the door.

"Uh, hello," said Josh uncertainly. "I came to see about Elmer."

"Elmer?" the man said quizzically. Then suddenly his face changed and his eyes lit up. "Ah! *Elmer!*" he said, opening the door wider still. "Come right in!" He smiled at them both.

This is really weird, thought Wally.

They went through the lobby and the man opened the inner doors to the small theater. About fifteen people were milling around, some walking about onstage. The thing Wally noticed first was a huge backdrop on which a woman was painting a farm scene—a horse, a cow, a barn, a field . . .

Josh stopped in his tracks and Wally could see that he had noticed too. The woman was trying to paint the horse's legs on the backdrop, only they were the strangest-looking legs Josh and Wally had ever seen.

"I could paint better than that," Josh whispered to Wally. "If someone would just give me a brush, I could paint that whole scene better than she's doing."

But the bearded man was saying, "Come on! Come on!" and then, "Jane, this young man is here to see about Elmer. I think we've found the grocer's sons."

And Josh and Wally found themselves being ushered onto the stage among a group of smiling faces. And there, looking almost as embarrassed as Josh himself, was Beth Malloy.

■ ■ ■ ■ ■ ■ ■ ■ ■ ■ ■

Eight

■

Hostage

Caroline could hardly believe her eyes. It had worked! Her plan had actually worked! Josh had gotten the message and he was just curious enough to come and find out who really, really liked him, as the note said. What she did not expect, however, was that Wally would show up too.

"Ladies and gentlemen," said the director to the rest of the cast, "I believe our prayers have been answered." Everyone clapped.

Josh stared at Beth, and Beth's face turned as pink as her sweater.

"You're Josh and Wally Hatford, aren't you?" the director asked. "All right, boys, you are going to be Elmer and Clyde. Josh, you're Elmer, and Wally, you're Clyde."

Wally was already shaking his head and moving backward, but Josh seemed hypnotized by the scenery.

"The horse is all wrong," he said, pointing.

Everyone turned and looked at the scenery. The artist sat back on her heels and looked at her painting, tipping her head to one side.

"It *is* wrong," she said, "but I don't know exactly why. I *told* them when they asked me to paint the set that I wasn't good at animals."

"Josh is!" cried Caroline quickly. "His pictures are all over the halls at school, and horses are one of the things he draws best."

"Josh," said the director, "we really, really need you. You only have a few lines in the play, and Wally just has to hang around onstage. But could you possibly consent to help paint the scenery too?"

Caroline held her breath. If the director couldn't find any boys to play the parts, she'd probably call the whole thing off, and there would go Caroline's chance to be in a real grown-up play. Any minute Josh and Wally would bolt. Any minute they would realize that she had put that note together. Any minute, in fact, Josh could pull it out of his pocket, walk over, and smush it in her face, just as the girls had rubbed snow in Jake's face the day before.

Except that Josh was still staring at the horse on the backdrop, and everyone was staring at Josh and waiting, and finally he said, "Yeah, but I'll have to do the cows over, too. There's something wrong with their legs."

"It's acrylic paint. You can paint right over my work," the woman said. "Oh, we do appreciate you, young man. We'll put your name on the program."

"Now!" said Jane, the director. "Let's have the scene where Elmer proposes to Annabelle," and she explained to Josh and Wally the parts they would play in the story—how the grocer's lazy sons would not help out on the farmer's land, but when Elmer met Annabelle, he changed his mind, and it was when the two families came together that the town of Buckman was born.

So everyone watched while Josh took Beth's hands and said, "Annabelle, I never thought I'd amount to much, but when I met you, everything changed."

And Beth, glancing shyly at Josh, then down at the floor, said, "With you by my side, Elmer, we can do anything."

All Wally had to do was sprawl in a corner and pretend to chew on a piece of clover.

"Perfect!" said the director.

At which point Caroline was to come out, stage left. While Elmer and Annabelle were still holding hands, she said to the audience, "If they think they're going to have a wedding without inviting me to be in the bridal party, just wait!" And she said it with such force, such style, that the rest of the players all clapped. All except Tracy Lee, her understudy, who glared at her from the first row.

When the rehearsal was over, Josh and Wally were the first ones out the door, though Josh did agree to come by after school the following evening and work on painting the set.

Beth seemed in a daze as she walked home beside Caroline.

"I can't believe what happened!" she kept saying. "What made Josh and Wally just walk in there and volunteer to be in that play?"

Caroline was about to tell her, but then she decided that had better be her secret. It was better for Beth to think that they were there because they wanted to be than that they had been tricked into coming. So she chirped, "You know, of all the Hatford boys, I think Josh is the nicest. Next to Peter, of course."

"Well, he's certainly a lot different from Jake," Beth agreed. "He's a good artist, too."

■

The following day at school, Wally seemed to be avoiding Caroline. Even when she poked him with her ruler and said, "Good morning, Clyde," he wouldn't turn around.

Uh-oh, Caroline thought. *I'd better not annoy him.* So she ignored him for the rest of the day, and that seemed just fine with Wally.

The girls had only been home twenty minutes that afternoon—a note from their mother said she was attending a meeting of the faculty wives—when there was a knock on the door and Caroline opened it to find Peter on their doorstep.

"Hi, Peter, come in," she said.

Peter was not smiling. He walked straight out to the kitchen and sat down on a chair. Then he glanced around the kitchen at Caroline and her sisters.

"Why did you put lima beans in our brownies?" he demanded of Caroline.

Aha! So the boys *had* noticed!

"Because," said Caroline, "you kidnapped me and held me hostage. If they had asked nicely, I might have baked them some brownies and done it right."

"They were yucky!" Peter complained. "We had to

dig out all the peas and lima beans and Jake was really mad!"

"Good!" said Caroline. "So was I."

Eddie, however, sat down at the table across from Peter and said, "You know, we can't quite figure out what's going on with your brothers. Are you guys friends with us or not? I thought you said your New Year's resolution was to be nicer to us."

"It was," said Peter. "We promised Mom we'd treat you like sisters, too, but Jake says you don't always have to treat sisters nice."

"I see!" said Eddie. "A loophole! Well, I guess if you treat us like sisters, we can treat you like brothers. Right?"

"I guess so," said Peter doubtfully.

Eddie exchanged looks with Beth and Caroline, and they knew she was up to something.

"Okay, I'll tell you what," Eddie continued. "You guys kidnapped Caroline and held her hostage, so we're going to kidnap you."

Peter's eyes opened wide.

"I don't know how to bake brownies!" he said, looking alarmed.

"Oh, you don't have to make them. We're just going to keep you here for a little while and give you treats!" Eddie said. "All you have to do is eat them. Get out the chocolate chips, Beth."

Beth opened the cupboard and reached for a package.

"O-kay!" said Peter, smiling.

"The only thing is, you have to promise to come

over here every few days and tell us everything your brothers are planning to do to us," said Eddie.

"Yeah," said Beth. "It's only fair."

"But you can't let them know about it, okay?" Eddie said. "If we're your sisters, then you have to be good to us and tell us everything. And every time you come, you get candy or cookies or ice cream or something."

"O-*kay*!" Peter said again.

Beth sat down on the other side of Peter, and Caroline opened the bag of chocolate chips.

"Now!" said Beth. "Did Josh tell you that he was going to be in a play?"

Peter nodded.

Caroline gave him a chocolate chip.

"Did he say I was in it too?" asked Beth.

"Uh-huh," said Peter.

Another chocolate chip.

"Did he say he liked me?" Beth went on, trying not to giggle.

Peter thought about it. "I think so," he said, and looked at the chocolate chips, waiting.

"What happened at your house last night?" Beth went on.

"Josh said he was in a play and had to hold hands with you and get married and Jake said he was crazy," Peter told them.

Caroline poured out a whole bunch of chips and pushed them across the table toward Peter.

■ ■ ■ ■ ■ ■ ■ ■ ■ ■ ■

Nine

Birthday Blues

"**Y**ou're going to do *what*?"

Mrs. Hatford was balancing the checkbook when Josh and Wally got back from the theater, and Mr. Hatford asked what they'd been doing.

"We're going to be in a play," Josh repeated. "I have to do it, I think, if I want to paint the scenery, and I *really* want to paint it. It covers the whole back of the stage, and it would be the first time outside of school that anyone has seen my paintings."

"Yeah, Mom, you should see the scenery they've got there now. The cows look like bathtubs with women's legs on them," put in Wally, eager to stand up for Josh and be the buddy of his older brother.

"Well, my goodness, that's something!" Mrs. Hatford declared. "Josh is going to paint the scenery for the play?"

"And he'll get his name on the program too," said Wally.

"Do we get to come and see you?" asked Peter.

That was the part Wally dreaded—that people would come and see them. "I guess so," he said miserably.

"It's all part of the grand celebration of Buckman's two hundredth anniversary," said Mr. Hatford, enjoying a cup of coffee over his newspaper. "They're thinking up all kinds of ways to celebrate. It's nice to see them making use of the old theater."

The only person who hadn't said anything yet was Jake. He was sprawled in front of the TV when Josh and Wally came in, but when they finally went upstairs, he followed. So did Peter.

"Are you guys nuts?" Jake asked as soon as they had all gathered in the twins' bedroom.

Josh looked uncomfortable. "Why?" he asked, getting out his Game Boy and pretending to play on his bed.

"Since when did you ever want to be in a play? How come you went off without telling me? What's going on?" Jake wanted to know.

Josh pretended he hadn't heard and frowned at the game in his lap.

Wally tried to help. "He really wants to paint the scenery. And he only has to say one line."

"Yeah? What?" asked Jake.

Josh went on frowning at the Game Boy, and Wally didn't know what to say. He waited.

"Well?" said Jake.

There didn't seem any point in not telling, because when the family came to see the play—the family and the whole town of Buckman, in fact—they'd hear Josh say it loud and clear.

" 'Annabelle, I never thought I'd amount to much, but when I met you, everything changed,' " Wally told him. "That's Josh's line."

"Oh, boy!" Jake yelled, throwing back his head in disgust. "Oh, boy!" Then he stopped yelling and stared at Josh. "Who do you have to say it to?"

"Annabelle," Wally said quickly, answering for Josh.

"Who's Annabelle?" Jake asked.

"Just some girl," Josh said.

"Well, you must be crazy," Jake told them. "I wouldn't get up in front of an audience and say that to a girl for a million dollars."

"I would," said Peter. "A million dollars is a lot of dollars."

"What do *you* have to do, Wally?" Jake asked.

"Nothing. Just hang around onstage."

"Man, I don't know what's happening to you guys. The Bensons move away and everyone goes nuts. I don't understand anything anymore," Jake complained.

"Well, I don't know what you're yelling about," Josh said suddenly. "You don't have to be in a play, so just shut up about it. If I want to paint scenery, that's my business. And who cares what I have to say to Beth if I get my name on the program for painting the set?"

Jake stared. "Beth? Beth Malloy? You're saying that

line to Beth Malloy?" He clutched his head in both hands and left the room. "Arrrrggggghhhh!" he yelled.

"I think she's nice," said Peter.

"I don't want to talk about it anymore," said Josh.

So Peter went back downstairs and Wally went to his room. He lay on his bed and stared at the crack in the ceiling. Things *were* changing; Jake was right. Wally wasn't sure whether it was a good change or a bad one, but things were certainly different than they'd been when the Bensons were here.

Plus the fact that in a few days he'd be ten years old. It seemed as though Wally had been waiting all his life to be ten, but now that it was almost here, he wondered if it would be as wonderful as he'd imagined.

Maybe twelve was the really big birthday celebration. Or what about sixteen?

His birthday came a little too soon after Christmas to suit him. Jake and Josh had their birthdays in April, and Peter didn't have his till August.

Mrs. Hatford didn't go in much for parties, but sometimes she said they each could invite a few friends to go bowling or something, or she'd take Wally and some of his friends to the movies, but she hadn't said anything yet about his birthday this year.

■

It was at breakfast the next morning that Mrs. Hatford mentioned the birthday. Actually, it was Mr. Hatford who said something. "Ellen, do you realize that Wally will be ten years old this weekend?"

"I was thinking of that yesterday," Mrs. Hatford

said, "because Jean Malloy was in the hardware store looking for a snow saucer for Caroline's birthday, and—"

"*Caroline's* birthday?" Wally asked.

"Yes, she's having a birthday the day after yours, and I said 'Why don't you come over this Saturday and we'll celebrate their birthdays together?' "

"*Mom!*" yelled Wally.

"They're not coming, are they?" asked Jake.

"Well, I don't see why not," Mrs. Hatford said, looking around uncertainly.

"Why did you invite them?" Wally bleated. "You could at least have asked me! I don't *want* to celebrate my birthday with Caroline."

"Ellen, you should have asked Wally first," said Mr. Hatford. "It's his birthday, after all."

Mrs. Hatford looked confused and upset. "Tom, it just seemed the least I could do, after all our boys have done to torment those girls."

Jake, Josh, and Wally groaned in protest.

"Besides," their mother went on. "It's our turn to have the Malloys here. We invited them at Thanksgiving, they invited us at Christmas, and now with two birthdays coming up on the exact same weekend, I thought . . ."

"Mom, Caroline is a year younger than I am! She's *precocious*! She'll only be nine. This is my tenth birthday, the only tenth birthday I'll ever have, and I don't want to spend it with the Crazie."

"That's what we call them," Jake explained. "Eddie, Beth, and Caroline—the Whomper, the Weirdo, and the Crazie."

Mr. Hatford finished his last bite of oatmeal and got up.

"Well, I've got mail to deliver. You'll have to work this out yourselves, but I think you went a little too far this time, Ellen."

"Tom, what can I do? I can't *un*invite them, can I?"

"I guess you can't," said Mr. Hatford as he went upstairs to brush his teeth.

Mrs. Hatford looked guiltily about the breakfast table.

"I'll tell you what, Wally," she said. "We'll just invite them over in the afternoon for cake and ice cream, and then we'll have our real celebration in the evening, and you can invite whomever you like. We'll have your official party then."

"Okay," said Wally, but he knew very well that if he had to spend the afternoon with the Malloys, being not only nice and friendly but polite as well, he might not feel like celebrating later at all.

Ten

■

Letter to Georgia

Dear Bill (and Danny, Steve, Tony, and Doug):

I mean it, if you guys don't come back soon, something terrible is going to happen. Do you know what's going on here?

1. *We had to make a New Year's resolution to be nice, friendly, and polite to the Malloy girls.*

2. *Josh is falling in love with Beth, I think, and is even in a play with her, and they're going to hold hands.*

3. *I have to be in the play too because Josh is.*

4. *I have to celebrate my birthday with Caroline, whose birthday is the day after mine.*

5. *We are all going nuts.*

Wally

Eleven

■

A Curious Celebration

"Mom!" yelled Caroline.

Mrs. Malloy looked anxiously around the dinner table. "Well, I just didn't know what to say," she confessed. "We were talking about the coincidence of you and Wally having birthdays only a day apart, and when she invited us over for cake and ice cream, it would have seemed terribly rude to say no."

"Caroline, it's not going to kill you," said Mr. Malloy. "You can have a regular celebration on Sunday, but there's no reason we can't go over to the Hatfords' for an hour on Saturday and wish Wally a happy birthday."

"Do we have to take him a present?" asked Eddie.

"Well, it seems the most friendly thing to do," Mrs. Malloy said.

"We *each* have to bring him a present?" wailed Beth.

"No, we'll find something we can give him from the whole family," said her mother. "It will be perfectly painless, I assure you."

"I doubt it," said Eddie.

It seemed to Caroline as though the Hatfords and the Malloys were destined to live overlapping lives as long as the Malloys stayed in Buckman. Whether this was bad or good, she wasn't sure, but she *was* sure she didn't want to share her birthday with Wally Hatford.

Nevertheless, she did not want to do one single thing that might affect the play, which was being advertised as *The Birth of Buckman*. If she insulted Wally, he might not come to rehearsals. If Wally dropped out of the play, Josh wouldn't come either. If Josh didn't come, they might not find a replacement, and if there were no grocer's lazy sons, the whole play might be called off and she herself would lose her chance for the performance of her life.

At school the next day, Caroline left Wally strictly alone. No poking him in the back with her ruler. No sticking him in the arm with her pencil. No blowing on the back of his neck. She did not call him Clyde either.

That evening she saw him at the Buckman Community Players, where he sat reluctantly in the back row of the theater and only went onstage when he had to. Josh, on the other hand, worked eagerly on the scenery, stopping only long enough to say his lines with Beth, and went immediately back to his painting.

"What do you think, Caroline? Do you think Josh

likes me?" Beth asked as the girls walked home together afterward.

It was hard to tell. It was obvious that Josh was
more interested in painting the scenery than in being
in the play, but still, if he didn't like Beth, not even a
little, he wouldn't hold hands with her in front of a
bunch of people, would he?

"Of course he likes you," said Caroline. She might
be only eight years old—well, almost nine—but Caroline knew perfectly well that if *Beth* didn't like Josh
a little, *she* wouldn't come to rehearsals.

The rehearsal had gone a little more smoothly this
time, the lines said with more expression. Most of the
lines were read by a narrator who was telling the story
of how a grocer and farmer got together to propose
the town of Buckman, but every so often the actors
would act out a little scene that the narrator was talking about.

The only people who hadn't seemed to be having
much fun were the understudies, who would have
liked to be main characters instead of townspeople.
Tracy Lee had looked at Caroline as though she
would be absolutely delighted if Caroline were to
break a leg.

∎

The next afternoon, Saturday, the Malloys walked
across the swinging bridge to the Hatfords' house and
knocked at the door.

Mrs. Malloy had bought a computer game for
Wally that he and his brothers could play, and she'd
also bought a gallon of French vanilla ice cream to go

with the chocolate chiffon cake that Mrs. Hatford had made for the birthday party.

"Oh, come in! Come in!" Mrs. Hatford said. "Wally, take their coats, will you, and put them upstairs on our bed?"

The Hatford boys were obviously freshly washed, combed, and dressed, and looked thoroughly uncomfortable. Beth and Josh glanced at each other and both blushed, Caroline noticed.

"Don't take your eyes off those guys for a minute," Eddie had warned as the girls had dressed for the party that afternoon. "After what Caroline did to their brownies, you can just bet they'll have some horrible trick up their sleeves."

"Like mud in the ice cream or cardboard in the cake," said Caroline. Nevertheless, she *was* the birthday girl, and she was wearing a gorgeous yellow dress that made her look and feel like a princess, and she decided that no matter what the Hatford boys did to annoy her, she would not allow them to ruin her birthday weekend.

"Well, Coach," said Mr. Hatford when they all sat down in the living room, "how do you think your team is going to size up in the play-offs?"

"It's been a pretty good season, actually," said Caroline's father. "We may never make it to the Big Ten, but we haven't done so bad in our division."

"Do you think you'll stay on here?" Mr. Hatford asked.

"I don't know yet. I guess it will depend on what

offers I get between now and summer," Mr. Malloy replied.

The talk shifted then to the Christmas season just past, and Mr. Hatford said it had been a record year for the post office.

"How long have you been carrying the mail?" Mrs. Malloy asked.

"Since I was twenty-two," Mr. Hatford told her. "Started out as a rural carrier only, way up in the hills. The one good thing about being a rural carrier, you never know what you'll find in people's mailboxes. Could be a piece of cake one day that somebody's left for you, and a kitten another. Folks'll do that, you know. Take a mess of kittens and go around putting 'em in folks' mailboxes. Somebody even put a skunk in a box once."

Everyone laughed.

"The only time he came home and I wouldn't let him in the house," said Mrs. Hatford, and everyone laughed again.

"Boys," said Mrs. Hatford, suddenly remembering what the visit was all about. "Don't you have a present for Caroline?"

"Oh, sure," said Wally. He went upstairs and returned with a flat box wrapped in gift paper from the hardware store. The Malloys, in turn, handed Wally his gift.

Somewhat awkwardly, Caroline and Wally both opened their gifts at the same time.

Wally seemed very pleased with his electronic game.

"Dragonia!" Jake and Josh said when they saw it. "Hey, that's a good one, Wally!"

"Thank you," Wally told the Malloys, surprised. "I think I'll like it."

Caroline opened her present then. It was a mirror, decorated with tiny ceramic dolls around the edge, each wearing the costume of a foreign country.

It was such a nice present that Caroline was shocked.

"So you can look at yourself all day if you want," Wally said.

Everyone laughed. Caroline was so pleased with the gift that she didn't mind.

"Well, I have coffee waiting. And cake and the Malloys' ice cream," Mrs. Hatford said.

"Chocolate chiffon cake, too!" said Josh, grinning a little at Beth.

"The kind you tossed in the river," added Jake, looking at Caroline.

Caroline blushed furiously, but everyone seemed to take it in good humor and they moved into the dining room for the refreshments.

"Watch the cake and ice cream," Eddie whispered. "I sure won't take the first bite."

Everyone took their places. The beautiful chocolate chiffon cake in the center of the table was cut into a dozen pieces, and a large piece was distributed to each plate. Mr. Hatford took the gallon of French vanilla that the Malloys had brought and put a large scoop of it on top of each piece. Then Mrs. Hatford poured coffee for the adults, pop for the kids, and everyone picked up their forks.

All the Hatfords took a bite. Mr. and Mrs. Malloy took a bite. They all said how delicious it was, and Caroline saw no reason not to eat it. After all, Mrs. Hatford had cut the pieces, not the boys. Mr. Hatford had dipped up the ice cream, not Jake. She took a large bite of cake and put it in her mouth. Absolutely delicious. Beth took the next bite, then Eddie. And soon surprised looks traveled between them as they all devoured their dessert and even wished there were more.

"This has been a lovely afternoon," Mrs. Malloy said, "but I'm afraid we must go. Caroline has invited some girls from school over for a little party tomorrow, so I'd better get ready."

"Same here," said Mr. Hatford. "I promised Wally I'd take him and his brothers bowling. We're delighted that you folks could stop by."

"We are too. Thanks for inviting us," said Mr. Malloy.

Wally, Jake, and Josh went upstairs and brought down all the coats. Each of the three boys helped one of the girls on with her parka, and they were all so polite that for once even Eddie was speechless.

As soon as they got out on the porch, Beth said, "I can't believe how nice they were." A sharp wind from the north caught them full in the face, and the three girls yanked up the hoods of their jackets.

Rat-a-tat-a-tat-a-tat!
Bing!
Pong!
Pop!

Bap!

Showers of something small and hard rained down on the floor of the porch. Cupfuls of something that had been nestled in their hoods.

"What in the world?" said Mrs. Malloy, turning to stare.

"Lima beans!" yelled the girls all together, and as they walked out to the street, they saw the boys waving at them from an upstairs window.

Twelve

■

P.S.

Dear Bill (and Danny, Steve, Tony, and Doug):

We got even with the girls. Mom did the dumbest thing. She invited the Malloys over for cake and ice cream just because my birthday and Caroline's are one day apart. Did you ever hear anything so dumb? If the county dogcatcher had a birthday next to mine, would anybody think to invite him?

We not only had to share our cake, but we had to be nice and polite too. We even had to carry their coats upstairs. Well, we were nice, all right. We gave them all our lima beans. I mean, all. Jake found a package in the cupboard, and we poured lima beans into the hoods of the girls' jackets. When they started home and flipped up their hoods, they got a shower of lima beans.

I'm sick of winter. You want our snow? You can have it. I'm sick of school, too. I'm sick of being nice to Caroline.

Please come back!

Wally

Dear Wally (and Jake and Josh and Peter):

Hey, don't feel so bad. It isn't so great down here either.

1. Yeah, we'll take your snow. Not only was there no snow at Christmas, there wasn't any snow at all! There will never be any snow here in Georgia!

2. Dad still hasn't made up his mind whether we're moving back or staying here. I think the worst thing of all is not knowing where we'll be.

3. I had a cavity and I hate the dentist down here. He doesn't believe in Novocain.

4. Remember that really cool teacher here in school, that Georgia peach? She's getting married, and she left right after Christmas.

If we come back and find that the Whomper, the Weirdo, and the Crazie have put ballerina wallpaper in our rooms, we will barf.

Bill

Thirteen

■

"Break a Leg"

It was almost time for Buckman's anniversary celebration. *The Birth of Buckman* was probably as good as it was going to get. The costume committee had helped each player fashion a costume that looked at least something like the way people were supposed to have dressed back around 1800. Josh had finished painting the set—one horse, three cows, a barn, a fence, and a field. And Beth and Josh had held hands so many times and looked into each other's eyes so often that they could do it quite naturally now, with only a minimum of blushing.

"You're all going to come, aren't you?" Caroline asked her family the day before the performance. "I want you all sitting in the first row. Are you going to send me flowers onstage for the curtain call?"

"Why? Are you dying as soon as the show is over?" her father asked, lifting a piece of bacon to his mouth and snapping off the end.

"Dad!" Caroline scolded. "Actresses always get bouquets of flowers at the curtain call."

Mr. and Mrs. Malloy studied their youngest daughter across the table.

"Sweetheart," said her mother, "there's a little something you should know. You are *not* the only actress in the play, you do not even have the leading role, and this is not Broadway. You are learning a lot of different roles these days, and I would strongly suggest that you practice the role of being humble."

Caroline bristled. She hated criticism. She knew she'd have to learn to take it from a director, but she didn't want to take it from her parents.

"Well, I have the lead role of all the *girls*!" she said confidently.

"*Excuse* me?" said Beth.

"Besides you, I mean," Caroline said hastily.

Mr. Malloy finished his bacon and glanced at his watch. "Why don't you accept the fact that you were lucky to get a part in a community play and that everyone's part is important, and stop looking for special favors?" he said.

Caroline pressed her lips together and didn't reply. She didn't want her family so disgusted with her that they wouldn't even come to the performance. Down in her heart of hearts, however, she knew that she was perhaps the most precocious child in Buckman and that some day, when she was a famous actress, people would be standing in line for her autograph.

She dressed for school and tried not to say anything else that would upset Beth. Eddie seemed restless, however. Plays did not interest her very much. She longed to be doing something more active, and baseball season still seemed a long way off.

But all that restraint on Caroline's part was a little too much, and when she slid into her seat behind Wally, she could not resist poking him a little with her ruler and saying, "Good morning, Clyde! Are *you* going to send me flowers?"

"Huh?" said Wally, turning around.

"Flowers! For being in the play."

"Why would I send you flowers?" said Wally, and faced forward again.

Poke, poke. This time she poked him with her pencil.

"What?" Wally snapped, turning again.

"Do you suppose we'll still be in plays together when we're in high school?"

"You mean *you'll* still be around when we're in high school?" Wally asked in despair.

"I don't know. I just mean if we are."

"No," said Wally. "I don't ever plan to be in a play again the rest of my entire life. And I will never, ever send you flowers."

"Oh," said Caroline.

■

It was cold at recess and Caroline's throat felt a little scratchy, so she stayed in the shelter of the door and didn't venture out into the yard. Actresses had to be careful of so many things. It was amazing all the things you had to think about when you became an actress.

"Class," said Miss Applebaum. "I hope you are all planning to go to the grand birthday celebration of our town tomorrow. Sometimes we think about history only in terms of our country—the leaders who made it great—and we forget that even little towns like ours have a history—somebody, sometime, had to start the ball rolling and think about what *our* community might become. Everyone who attends one of the festivities this weekend will get an extra ten points for the unit. And that includes the play, *The Birth of Buckman,* in which two members of our class will star—Wally Hatford and Caroline Malloy."

What does she mean, mentioning Wally! Why, he doesn't even have any lines! Caroline thought. She started to stand up and take a bow, and then remembered what her mother had said about humility and decided she'd better stay seated.

■

Everyone was excited at rehearsal that night, because it was the final rehearsal before the performance and the players came in costume. Caroline wore a silver brooch at the collar of her high-necked blouse, and Mrs. Malloy piled Caroline's dark hair on top of her head and fastened it with a tortoiseshell comb.

Beth, however, looked even more beautiful in a long, soft blue dress with lace on the sleeves. A little spray of blue artificial flowers was tucked into her blond hair.

It was almost enough, Eddie declared, to make *her* want to be in the play so that *she* could look beautiful, but not enough to make her go onstage and act stupid.

Caroline was very quiet as Mr. Malloy drove them to the old theater that evening. What she was feeling was tired. All the excitement and stress of the past two weeks, all the evening rehearsals, were beginning to show, and she didn't have her usual spunk. But when she got up on the stage and saw Tracy Lee watching from the seats below, just waiting to spring onstage and take over if anything happened to Caroline, she performed with every ounce of energy she had, and the director told her it was one of her finest performances.

"Just do that well tomorrow night," she told her, "and you will never have done better."

The set was finished, the paint was dry, the old-time furniture collected and placed onstage, and as all the players left the theater that night, the men and women laughingly called to each other, "Break a leg! Break a leg!"

Caroline could not believe her ears! What a terrible thing to say, she thought.

But when she told her mother, who had come to pick her up in the car, Mrs. Malloy said, "Actually, that's a good-luck wish among theater folk, Caroline. They don't actually mean they wish it to happen. It's sort of a superstition that if you *wish* for something to happen, or say that you do, then it won't. It's like a good-luck charm to ward off misfortune."

"Oh!" said Caroline, and felt very important that she was actually being around theater people now, hearing their talk, and being a part of it all.

∎

But the next morning, Saturday, Caroline awoke with a sore throat and a headache. She drank a little orange juice and insisted she was only tired. When she fell asleep on the couch after lunch, Mrs. Malloy made her go up to bed for a nap so that she would feel better before the long show that evening.

There were to be speeches that afternoon and a high-school band concert, and Caroline wanted to go—wanted to tell everyone she met to be sure to come back downtown that evening to see her perform in *The Birth of Buckman.* But Mrs. Malloy said she had to rest for the play, so Caroline gratefully crawled under the covers and went to sleep.

When Mrs. Malloy went to wake her at five to get dressed for the performance, she found Caroline's cheeks burning red and a light rash on her face and arms. Caroline could hardly open her eyes, and when she tried to talk, her voice was husky.

Mrs. Malloy quickly got the thermometer.

"One hundred and four!" she said. "Caroline, I'm sorry, but you can't be in the play this evening. You are much too sick."

"Mother!" Caroline wailed, tears welling up in her eyes.

"I'm going right to the phone and call the director. Tracy Lee will have to take over, and I'll have your father run your costume over to her house. I'm so sorry, honey. I'll see if I can't reach Dr. Raskin, too."

She went downstairs to call.

"Mother!" Caroline wailed again. Her voice sounded like the bleating of a sick calf. There was a thump on the floor. Then another.

Beth and Eddie and Mr. and Mrs. Malloy went to the foot of the stairs.

Caroline was standing at the top, trying to get one of her pajama-clad legs into her long black skirt.

"I—I've got to be in the play!" Caroline croaked, her face pinker still. "Don't call the director! Don't! I don't want Tracy Lee to wear my clothes! I don't want her to be Beulah!"

She tried to put the other leg in the skirt, hobbling about on one foot, but at that moment she lost her balance and came tumbling halfway down the stairs, determined, it seemed, to almost, but not quite, "break a leg."

■ ■ ■ ■ ■ ■ ■ ■ ■ ■ ■ ■

Fourteen

■

The Birth of Buckman

The Hatfords were preparing to go to the theater. Josh and Wally were dressed up like boys of long ago. Josh was in a three-piece suit and a shirt with a high collar that felt like a rope around his neck. Wally wore a flannel shirt and baggy pants with suspenders. Josh wore a straw hat, Wally a leather cap, and they were each so clean and scrubbed that Wally complained his ears squeaked.

"Wait till you see the set, Mom!" Josh kept saying. "The stage manager just turned the backdrop over and let me paint a whole new scene. It really looks like a field now, with the animals in the back smaller and the ones in the front bigger."

"And they don't have women's legs on them, either," Wally said. "Everything looks real."

"This is an exciting day for you, Josh—almost like having your paintings in a gallery," Mrs. Hatford said. "I've invited all my friends to come."

What Josh wished, of course, was that all *his* friends would come to see the set, and then leave before he had to hold hands with Beth Malloy and say those sappy lines.

On the other hand, if he had to say them at all, he'd rather say them to Beth than any other girl he could think of.

Wally, however, was only thankful that he didn't have to hold hands with anybody onstage, *especially* with a girl. Thankful he didn't have to say anything, either. The only reason he was in this stupid play at all was because Josh wanted company and Wally wanted to be his buddy.

Jake hadn't even wanted to go watch. He said he saw his brothers acting dumb every day, why would he want to go to a theater and see them act dumb onstage?

But Mrs. Hatford said this was a family affair, and if he didn't care enough for his brothers to come and watch their performance, then he could wash all the supper dishes she'd left in the sink. Jake put on his coat and cap. Everyone piled into Mr. Hatford's Jeep, the one he used when he delivered rural mail, and drove the few blocks downtown, Peter chattering happily in the backseat.

At the theater, Wally and Josh used the stage entrance while the rest of the family went in the door at the front.

The other cast members were nervously putting on makeup, combing their hair, and straightening the sleeves of their costumes.

Mrs. Malloy was brushing Beth's hair, tucking little

flowers into the headband across the top. Wally heard her say, "I won't be able to stay long, dear. Caroline's sleeping, so as soon as you say your lines, I'm going to zip back home. The doctor thought he could get there about nine."

"That's okay, Mom," Beth said. "I understand."

"Is Caroline sick?" Wally asked, walking over.

"Yes, poor thing. She is just beside herself that she can't be in the play. She looked forward to it so much," Mrs. Malloy told him. "But we took her costume over to Tracy Lee, and I know she'll do a fine job."

Man, oh, man! thought Wally, would Caroline ever be unbearable when she came back to school.

When the lights dimmed, a banjo player came onstage and played a lively tune, and then a spotlight shone on the narrator, who was sitting on a high stool over on the left side of the stage. He was telling the story of Buckman, about the farmer who had only daughters and the grocer who had only sons, and how one day they had talked about incorporating their little community and making it a town.

As he mentioned various events and conversations, the spotlight would jump to the players who had crept onstage. They would say their few lines, and then the spotlight would go off again and the narrator would continue. The person who was operating the spotlight, however, was obviously new at the job, for sometimes the spot of light would shine on absolutely nothing while a voice came from somewhere else onstage. Once, the spotlight fell on an actor's shoe and never did make it up to his face, and everyone laughed.

When Caroline was to come on as Beulah, Tracy Lee grandly made her entrance, wearing Caroline's clothes. When she said, "In fact, why not name it *Beulah,* after *me*?" the audience laughed loudly, and Tracy Lee looked pleased.

A few scenes later, Josh and Beth stood onstage holding hands. Wally was sitting on an overturned bucket, chewing a piece of clover—or what was supposed to be clover. He heard Jake give a soft groan of disgust down in the first row when Josh said, "Annabelle, I never thought I'd amount to much, but when I met you, everything changed."

And Wally heard Mrs. Malloy sigh when Beth looked up into his eyes and said, "With you by my side, Elmer, we can do anything."

It was at that moment the spotlight turned to the right, where Beulah would tiptoe onstage and whisper to the audience, "If they think they can have a wedding without inviting *me* to be in the bridal party, they're in for a surprise!" Tracy Lee started to step out in Caroline's long black skirt and blouse, when suddenly an arm reached out and yanked her back, and there came Caroline in her coat and pajamas, her face flushed, her hair disheveled. Her voice was as raspy as a rusty saw, and she bleated, "If they think they can have a wedding without . . . with . . . uh . . . ," and she stumbled about awkwardly onstage.

The audience gasped.

"Caroline!" came a stage whisper from behind the

curtain, and another arm reached out and tried to grab her.

"Caroline!" cried Mrs. Malloy from the second row, and immediately got up and exited through the little door beside the stage.

"Let go!" Caroline was crying, flailing at the hands—three of them now—that were trying to grab her. "I'm Beulah! Please! I'll be the sickly daughter, then! I *am* sick! Oh, please let me be in the play!"

But at that point Mrs. Malloy herself stepped on-stage, encircled her feverish daughter in her arms, and whisked her away.

Wally could not believe his eyes. The fake clover fell out of his mouth.

Beth and Josh continued to hold hands, staring after Caroline, and the narrator shakily began reading again. Offstage, Wally could hear Caroline's muffled protests as she was led outside, and Tracy Lee's sobs, but the show went on, as it always must, and when it was all over, the audience broke into loud applause.

Josh, Wally, and Beth stood in the wings talking after the final curtain.

"I was *so* embarrassed!" Beth kept saying.

"It's not your fault," Josh told her. "Everyone knows that."

"Everyone knows it was my sister, though! She was acting half crazy. She must be even sicker than we thought!"

Tracy Lee marched by with fire in her eyes and said to Beth, "I never want to be in a play with your sister again. She just has to have all the attention, doesn't she? Well, she got it, and I hope she's satisfied."

But family members were crowding backstage now. The art teacher from school was there.

"Josh, is this true? The program said you painted the set. It's wonderful!"

"Yeah. It was lots of fun," Josh told her.

"Wonderful job, Josh," said another teacher.

"Just great," said Mr. Hatford.

Wally was glad that the play was over and that neither he nor Josh had goofed up. He was glad that everyone had liked the set. But there was another feeling he had never, ever felt before, and he could hardly believe he felt it. He was really, truly a little bit sorry for Caroline Malloy.

■ ■ ■ ■ ■ ■ ■ ■ ■ ■ ■

Fifteen

■

The Awakening

Caroline had only the dimmest recollection of what had happened. She vaguely remembered getting out of bed when she heard her family leaving for the theater, but she had no memory at all of pulling on her coat and boots.

She did remember that it had been cold outside, and that it had seemed a very long three blocks to the theater. But when she went in the stage entrance, she stood by the radiator a minute, which warmed her, and then she heard Beth and Josh saying their lines, and after that . . . she only remembered how bright the lights had seemed and how dark the audience, and all the hands reaching . . . reaching . . . to pull her back.

Mrs. Malloy was sitting by her bed when she opened her eyes again, and so was Dr. Raskin.

"It sure looks like strep," the doctor was saying.

"We'll take a throat culture to be sure, but I'd bet my last dollar." Caroline gagged when he swabbed her throat. It was so very sore.

"I know you're feeling rotten, Caroline," the doctor went on, "but I've given you a shot of penicillin and we're working on that fever." He looked at Mrs. Malloy. "She should be better in a day or two. Call me if you need to."

And with a pat on Caroline's knee, he picked up his bag and left the room.

Mrs. Malloy sat down again beside the bed.

"I feel awful," Caroline whispered huskily.

"I know," said her mother.

"My head hurts and my throat's on fire."

"I know," her mother said.

"And I had the most awful dream! I dreamed that I went onstage in my pajamas."

"I know," Mrs. Malloy said again.

Caroline closed her eyes and slept once more, and the next time she opened them, Beth and Eddie were sitting beside the bed.

"Hey, Sleeping Beauty, how are you feeling?" asked Eddie.

"Awful," said Caroline. "I keep having this dream that I'm going onstage in my pajamas."

"That was a nightmare, all right," said Beth. "But it could have been worse. You could have walked on naked as a lightbulb."

Caroline tried to sit up and braced herself on one elbow.

"It didn't really *happen,* did it?" she croaked.

Beth and Eddie looked at each other.

"She's going to find out eventually," Eddie whispered. "Might as well tell her."

Beth looked at Caroline. "Yes, it really happened. You came onstage in your pajamas and boots and coat and said you were Beulah."

"Or the sickly daughter, either one," added Eddie.

Caroline's eyes widened in horror. "Then . . . Then there *were* lights in my eyes, and there *were* hands reaching out, trying to pull me back."

"You bet," said Eddie. "The most excitement Buckman has had all year. But don't worry. Everyone realized you were simply out of your head."

Caroline fell back on her pillow. "I'll never go out of the house again! I'll never be able to face anyone, Eddie!" And she started to cry.

"We shouldn't have told her," Beth whispered.

"And have her find it out from the Hatfords? Are you nuts?" asked Eddie.

"I want to be home-schooled!" Caroline wailed. "I want to go to a convent! I want to go back to Ohio—*now*!"

Mrs. Malloy came into the room and, with a stern look at Beth and Eddie, sent them scurrying. Then she sat down beside Caroline and took her hand.

"Caroline," she said, "the first thing actresses have to learn is to *use* the things that happen to them, even the awful things. Don't try to throw it away. I know you're embarrassed, but whenever you need to act embarrassed in a play in the future, you will know how that feels. You'll remember this moment, and remembering will help your cheeks grow pink, your pulse to race. Keep every sad or angry or fearful or embarrassing thing that ever happens to you in your memory bank so that you can draw on it when you need to."

Mrs. Malloy was the only one who understood.

"Thanks, Mom," said Caroline. It didn't make the humiliation less real, but it did help to think that maybe all great actresses had to go through this from time to time, and that someday, when she was on Broadway, people would forget all about tonight and remember her only as a famous actress.

But that was a long way off. Right now she had to think about facing her friends at school. Worse yet, she had to face the Hatfords.

■

It was Thursday before she could go to school. Wally had been bringing her homework by and leaving it with Mrs. Malloy. But now the time had come to face the class. The first day back she asked Eddie to walk in front of her so no one could see her coming, and Beth to walk in back so no one could see her from behind.

Still, she felt absolutely sick inside, and as soon as she walked into her classroom, she knew that everyone was looking at her, even the teacher, as though at any moment she might stand up and do something crazy.

Wally, in fact, kept leaning forward in his seat as if she might go berserk and take a bite out of his shoulder or something.

But Caroline tried to remain calm, and when Wally finally turned around and said, "Welcome back from the crazy house," Caroline replied, "You're right. I was positively out of my head with fever. It was the highest fever a girl has ever had and survived, and if it had been any higher I would have died."

"No kidding?" said Wally, his eyes growing larger.

"In fact," said Caroline, who couldn't stop herself, "I didn't have any shoes on, just boots, when I walked to the theater, and I couldn't even feel the cold. If there had been hot coals onstage, I could have walked across them and not even felt it. When a person is in as feverish a state as I was, she could stick knives in her arms and pierce her tongue and not feel a single thing. In fact—"

"Caroline, do you have something you'd like to share with the whole class, or can your private conversation wait until recess?" the teacher asked.

"Uh . . . it can wait," said Caroline.

But when Miss Applebaum began writing on the blackboard, Caroline leaned forward and whispered in Wally's ear, "In fact, I just may get my name in the *Guinness Book of World Records* for having the highest known temperature of any nine-year-old who lived to tell about it."

Sixteen

■

War

It seemed as though January might end peacefully. Caroline, Wally noticed, was quieter than usual. Josh noticed that Beth was kinder and more polite. Eddie, Jake reported, seemed as though she might be friendly after all.

The temperature dropped to the low twenties, and the Buckman River completely froze over, bringing out sleds and ice skates. Skaters glided down one side of Island Avenue, under the road bridge that led to the business district, and back up the river on the other side, their breath frosty in the sunny, crisp air.

Then it snowed—wonderful snow, excellent snow, the kind that packed a powerful snowball.

No one knew how it happened, but the peace didn't last.

The battle didn't start with Beth and Josh.

It didn't start with Caroline and Wally.

It didn't even start with Jake and Eddie, and it certainly didn't start with Peter.

All Wally knew was that he and his brothers were standing on the swinging bridge looking down at the Malloy girls ice-skating on the river below, and the next minute Caroline and her sisters were frantically building a snow fort on their side of the river as though they suspected the boys were up to no good. Every so often the girls shot suspicious glances their way.

"What did *we* do?" asked Josh. "Why are they glaring at us?"

"Who knows? Who cares? But they aren't building a fort to play house in," said Jake excitedly. "You build a fort for war!"

"Yeah!" said Wally. "It sure looks like war, all right." From where he was standing, he could see Beth and Eddie rolling big balls of snow down the bank on their side of the river and stacking them one on top of the other. Caroline, meanwhile, appeared to be making snowballs.

"Okay!" said Jake excitedly. "Let's fight!"

The boys ran to their end of the swinging bridge, went slipping and sliding down the bank, and began building a fort on *their* side of the river.

"Hey! Look what the guys are up to!" Wally heard Eddie shout. "I *told* you they were probably planning something back there on the bridge. We'll settle this once and for all." She picked up a large stick and went sliding out to the center of the river, where she scratched a long line in the ice.

"All right, you guys," she yelled. "Everything on

this side of the line is our territory. Everything on the other is yours. Don't cross the line and you won't get—"

Plop!

A snowball hit her on the shoulder.

At that, Beth and Caroline shrieked like savages and came swarming out of their fort. Suddenly the air was filled with snowballs going in both directions—some hitting their targets, some smashing on the ice, all of them accompanied by whoops and yells.

Every so often both camps retreated for a time to make more snowballs or repair their forts, and the walls grew even higher. Peter and Wally were busily making peepholes so that they could see out, in case Eddie got it in her crazy head to run over and stuff a snowball down somebody's neck.

They stayed until dusk set in and it was too dark to see anymore. Then they went home, half frozen but eager to continue the war.

After dinner that evening, the boys gathered as usual in Jake and Josh's bedroom, and while Peter absently ran his Matchbox cars along one windowsill, then another, the boys discussed their battle strategy.

"Let's go out and dump boiling water on their snow fort," said Wally.

"Naw. That would take too long. You'd have to keep carrying kettle after kettle," said Jake. "I think we should just go over and knock it down."

"Then they'll come over and knock ours down," said Josh.

"Not without a fight, they won't," said Jake. "Come on. Let's go."

Mrs. Hatford, however, came upstairs just then to remind Peter to take a bath, so Wally and the twins decided to go without him.

"Let's wait another fifteen minutes to be sure the girls aren't out there, and then we'll sneak over," Jake said. And they went downstairs to watch TV while they waited.

Finally they put on their jackets and caps and mittens and went outside. From the road the deserted ice gleamed in the light from the streetlamp. Wally could see a lone skater far down the river, going around a curve.

"I don't know," said Josh as they turned their feet sideways and started down the bank. "It does seem sort of a shame to tear their fort down. It has turrets and everything. It looks like a castle."

"Ha!" said Jake as they reached the bottom. "If they were out here right now, don't you think they'd be tearing down ours? You think they'd just walk across the ice and admire it? You think—"

Pow!

Biff!

Bop!

Whop!

The Hatfords were ambushed from their own fort. With bloodcurdling yells, Eddie, Beth, and Caroline rose up from inside the boys' fort, lobbing snowball after snowball, then ducking down when the boys returned their fire.

The boys retreated up the bank to rethink their strategy.

"How did they know we were coming?" Wally

panted. "They couldn't have been waiting out here all this time!"

"I don't know, but it sure looks like a setup to me," said Josh.

"Peter!" the three boys said together.

They stomped across the road and into the house. In single file, they marched up the stairs. There was still water in the bathtub. There was a wet towel on the floor. There were wet footprints leading from the bathroom, past the phone in the hallway, and on into Peter's room.

Jake opened Peter's door. Peter was lying motionless in his bed, one arm and one leg thrown over the side. His eyes were closed and he was breathing deeply. He looked too innocent for words.

The three boys did a little homework, and then, with their parents putting up shelves in the basement, they slipped on their coats again, their caps and mittens, and went back out for the third time that day.

Carefully they looked about. They walked out to the middle of the swinging bridge so that they could see down inside their fort. In the light from the streetlamp, they could see nothing. They crossed the river and slid down the bank by the girls' fort, then scouted out the area. Up on the hill they could see lights from the Bensons' old house. But there were no girls anywhere to be seen.

Wally felt slightly better about tearing down the girls' fort now that they had been ambushed, but Josh still seemed to hesitate. "They didn't really do anything to us, you know," he said. "If we hadn't come out here to knock down their fort in the first place, we wouldn't have run into them."

"Hey! It's all in fun! This is what brothers and sisters do!" Jake said.

He drew back one leg and kicked the girls' fort. A huge ball of snow on the bottom gave way. The wall crumbled, the turret landing in a heap at his feet.

It *was* sort of fun to watch the turrets fall, Wally decided as he slid around on the ice to the other end of their fort and pushed. The second turret exploded on the ice.

After that it was just a matter of pushing down the rounded hunks of snow and stepping on them, until the fort was nothing more than a pile of scattered snow on the ice.

"I wish we had a flag," said Jake.

"Why?" asked Wally.

"So we could prop it up on the pile—let the girls know we were here."

"I think they'll figure it out pretty fast," said Josh. "Who else would do this to them?"

"Yeah, but it would be fun to leave our mark somehow."

"We could do what dogs do," Wally suggested. "We could pee on it."

The twins turned and stared at him.

"You're really weird, Wally, you know?" said Jake.

Seventeen

■

The Traitor Returns

As soon as Caroline got Peter's phone call, she and her sisters hurried down to the river and hid in the Hatfords' fort. And as soon as the ambush of the boys was over and they returned home, Beth said, "You know they'll just come back and tear down our fort, don't you?"

"Of course!" said Eddie. "We're only going to stay here in the house until we're sure they've had time enough to do it. Then we'll go back down to the river, take *their* fort apart, and put it up on their front porch."

Caroline squealed with delight. This was one of the best tricks yet!

The girls took off their gloves and laid them over the radiator to dry.

"I spent a lot of time shaping those turrets, though," said Beth. "Our fort looked like a castle."

"The Hatfords probably *enjoy* being destructive! They *enjoy* tearing things down," said Eddie.

"Not Josh, though. I can't imagine *he'd* enjoy it very much," Beth mused.

"You'd be surprised!" said Eddie.

A half hour later the girls went out again. Just as they suspected, their snow fort had been demolished.

"Never mind," said Eddie, leading them across the ice to where the boys' sturdy fort stood guarding their side of the river. "Let's go!"

Following their plan, Caroline climbed up the bank and waited at the top. Beth climbed halfway up, and Eddie began the careful demolition of the fort. The idea was to move the whole thing, ball by ball, but the snow was so heavy that only the smaller hunks could be lifted. Eddie picked up a ball of snow and passed it carefully to Beth, who passed it to Caroline, who set it at the top of the bank. The work was slow, but finally at least half of the fort, minus one or two pieces that had crumbled along the way, had been moved.

"Whew!" Beth panted. "I've got to rest a minute, Eddie. This is *hard*. Why don't you ever get an easy idea?"

"You can only take a minute," said Eddie. "If we don't get home pretty soon, Dad will come looking for us. It's almost Caroline's bedtime."

They took a brief rest, and then, very, very quietly, they carried the hunks of snow across the road, up the sidewalk, and up the steps to the Hatfords' front porch. Eddie could carry whole balls of it herself, but it took both Caroline and Beth to carry one. They set to work reconstructing the fort right in front of the door, so that when the Hatfords came out the following morning, they would find themselves facing a wall of snow. One lump of snow . . . another . . . another . . .

Suddenly the porch light came on. In panic the girls flattened themselves against the house, holding their breath. Out of the corner of her eye, Caroline could see Mrs. Hatford peering out a side window. The snow fort, however, was not visible from that window, and a minute later the light went off again and the girls could hear Mrs. Hatford's footsteps retreating back down the front hallway.

"Whew!" said Beth, one hand on her chest. "Eddie, what would we have said if she'd come out?"

"I don't know, but we've got to hurry!" Eddie insisted. "Try not to make a sound."

The second row of snow was piled onto the first, then the third, igloo fashion, until finally the wall of snow blocking the front door was almost five feet high. All it would take was a single hard push to knock it down, of course, but they weren't trying to keep anyone from getting out. They were only trying to give them—namely Jake, Josh, Wally, and Peter— the surprise of their lives—a taste of their own medicine.

"What now?" asked Beth.

"Nothing," said Eddie. "Now we go home, and tomorrow we pretend that nothing out of the ordinary happened. We pretend we didn't even look at our own fort, didn't even realize it was gone."

Beth, however, didn't move. Looking as mischievous as Caroline was supposed to have looked in the play, she tentatively put one finger on the doorbell.

Caroline looked from Beth to Eddie.

Eddie began to grin. "Okay," she said.

"One . . . two . . . three . . . *go*!" Beth said, pressing the doorbell hard, and she and her sisters went sailing off the porch, across the yard, and tumbled down the bank toward the bridge.

They lay in the snow, their heads barely peeping up over the bank.

The porch light came on again, and they could hear the door opening.

"Hey!" came Wally's voice. "Hey! Jake! Josh! Come here!"

There was the sound of running feet, Jake's bellow, Mr. Hatford's whistle, and Mrs. Hatford's exclamations.

"Who in the world did this?" said Mrs. Hatford. "What do they think it is? Halloween?"

"Can we get out?" asked Wally, and the girls giggled when they heard the worry in his voice.

And then the snow wall came tumbling down, and Wally, Jake, and Josh ran to the edge of the porch in their stocking feet and looked around.

Silently the girls went on across the bridge, and then they linked arms and sang as they climbed the hill toward home.

■

Mr. Malloy was watching TV when his daughters came in. "Where have you been?" he asked. "You look as though you've been ice-skating! It's almost nine o'clock!"

"We've been having so much fun out on the ice!" Caroline said, winking at Eddie. "We just couldn't make ourselves stop."

"Girls!" called their mother from the dining room, where she was looking through a brochure of oil paintings, "I want you to see something."

The girls slipped off their jackets and walked into the next room. Mrs. Malloy pointed to a painting of the Appalachian Mountains in snow and fog. "I'm thinking of buying this painting from a gallery in Elkins—if not this exact picture, maybe one like it. I thought it would look especially nice over there above the buffet. What do you think?"

The girls came around behind her chair and looked at the picture.

"I like the fog," said Beth.

"I like the snow," said Caroline.

"I like the mountains," said Eddie. "Go ahead and buy it, Mom."

"I think this artist does wonderful work," Mrs. Malloy said, "but sometimes paintings look better on canvas than they do in a brochure and sometimes they look worse. I'll just have to see for myself."

"Does this mean we'll be staying in Buckman? I mean, are you buying pictures to go in this house?" asked Beth.

"I have no idea where we'll be come August," her mother told her. "But wherever we are, I think this painting might be gorgeous on any wall. You girls get to bed now. It's late."

The girls went upstairs, smiling to themselves. Their parents didn't suspect a thing.

"*That* will teach the guys to mess around with us," said Eddie.

"*That* will earn us a little respect," said Beth. "They'll *never* guess we lifted all that heavy snow and carried it up to their porch."

"We are totally, positively amazing!" said Caroline. "The magnificent Malloy sisters strike again!"

■

"I suppose you thought that was funny," Wally said to Caroline the next day as he slid into his seat at school.

"Funny, and extremely clever," smiled Caroline. "We're not just *girls,* Wally! We're *professionals*! We are so professional at being girls that we can outfox a boy any day, any time, any season. We can outgirl a boy before he even knows what hit him! Just think, Wally Hatford, we are something that you and your brothers can *never* be—wonderful, glorious, intelligent, adventurous, magnificent girls!"

She threw out her arms in a grand gesture and whacked Miss Applebaum, who happened to be coming up the aisle passing out their book reports.

"Oh! I'm sorry!" Caroline gasped.

"Could we have a little less grandeur, Caroline, do you think?" said her teacher.

■

Peter came over after school.

"Do I get some cookies?" he asked.

"Do you get *cookies*? How about a whole handful?" said Beth, leading him out to the kitchen.

She had already started a batch of double-chocolate-chunk cookies, her own special creation with little bits of coconut in them, and they were almost ready to take out of the oven.

"You really *are* a baker, aren't you!" Peter said admiringly.

"Yep. I think I'll go to culinary school or something," said Beth. "You know what I'll call my bakeshop when I get one, Peter? Malloy's Masterpieces, maybe. Or Beth's Breads or just Breads and Brownies or something. How does that sound?"

"It sounds wonderful!" said Peter. "I know what *I* want to be, too."

"What?"

"A spy! Or a detective."

"Hey, you'd make a great spy," Beth told him.

"You put that snow up on our porch, didn't you?" Peter went on. "Jake was really mad!" He watched as Beth opened the oven door. Eddie and Caroline came out in the kitchen too, and they all waited for the first batch to cool.

"So what happened?" asked Caroline.

"Dad made us clean it all off this morning before we went to school," Peter said.

"Aw, poor you!" said Caroline.

Eddie poured Peter a glass of milk. "Well, who knocked down *our* snow fort? *We* were mad!" she said.

Peter waited till a saucer with two large cookies sat in front of him, and then he said, "How many cookies do I get if I tell you something else?"

"All you can eat!" Caroline said quickly, picking up a cookie herself and blowing on it.

"Jake and Josh and Wally are going to sneak out

of school early tomorrow and go to the swinging bridge and build a big wall of snow so *you* can't go across, and then they're going to hit you with snowballs."

"Peter, you're a wonderful brother to us," said Eddie, exchanging looks with her sisters. "Give him another cookie, Caroline!"

■

The next morning while the girls were eating breakfast, Eddie said, "Okay, I've got it. When school's out, we don't come home the usual way; we walk down to the business district and use the road bridge to get to Island Avenue. The boys can wait at the end of the swinging bridge all night if they want to, but we'll be home having cocoa, laughing our heads off."

And they broke into laughter right then.

■

It began snowing a little before noon, however, and the next time Caroline looked out the window of her classroom, the flakes were coming down so thick and fast, they looked like giant white flowers. By two o'clock, several inches had accumulated on the window ledges, and the wind had picked up.

The principal's voice sounded over the school intercom.

"Students," he said, "there's a sudden winter storm warning for this area, and we have decided to close school an hour early—"

Every classroom erupted in cheers.

"You are all to go directly home, unless you have specific instructions as to where else to go in an emergency. The forecasters are predicting a foot of snow with gusting winds, and I repeat: all students are to go directly home."

All the kids in Caroline's class hurried to get their coats, laughing excitedly and staring out the hall windows at the approaching blizzard. The sky was gray and looked like broiling broth in a kettle.

"Have a nice snowdrift!" Wally said to Caroline.

"Have a nice avalanche," she replied.

"Have a good frostbite," said Wally.

"Same to you," said Caroline.

There was no need for the girls to take the road bridge back to Island Avenue because, with the coming storm, everyone was intent on simply getting home. The snow seeped into their sneakers. Out on the road, cars were already sliding about, skidding when they tried to stop and acting crazy.

The swinging bridge creaked and swayed as the girls made their way across, and they had to keep brushing snow from their faces so they could see. They made their way up the hill behind their house and let themselves in the back door.

There were no sounds from inside, however. No smell of hot cocoa waiting. No music. No rustling sounds coming from their mother's desk.

"Mom?" Caroline called.

No answer.

Beth went upstairs to check but soon came down again. "She's not here," she said. "I can't find any note. She almost always leaves a note."

"And her car's gone," said Eddie. "Look at the calendar. Maybe she had an appointment."

Caroline went to the little study off the living room and checked Mrs. Malloy's engagement calendar.

Noon, it said. *Fisher's Gallery, Elkins.*

Caroline looked at the desk clock. It was already half past two, and Elkins was thirty miles away.

Eighteen

■

Lost . . .

"We're out of cookies!"

Peter's bellow filled the house.

"Then eat crackers or something. Don't stand there shouting!" Wally told him.

But Peter was indignant. "Why don't we ever have cookies like the Malloys do? Yesterday they had coconut cookies with big hunks of chocolate in them! The day before that it was peanut butter."

Jake, Josh, and Wally came to the doorway of the kitchen and looked at Peter.

"How do *you* know?" asked Josh.

"They gave me some."

The boys continued to stare.

"Do you mean you go over there every day and they give you cookies?" asked Jake.

Peter nodded. "Big ones, too! And sometimes they're still warm!"

Jake sat down at the table next to Peter. Wally and Josh sat down across from him.

"Uh-oh," Peter murmured.

"Okay, tell us everything," said Josh.

Peter pressed his lips together and thrust himself against the back of his chair, arms folded across his chest.

"Listen, Peter, the Malloy sisters don't just invite you over for cookies every day for nothing," said Josh.

"I won't tell!" Peter declared.

"Tell what?" asked Wally.

"How they kidnapped me."

"They *kidnapped* you?"

"I won't tell because they let me go," said Peter.

"Yeah, they kidnapped you and fed you cookies and let you go if you did *what*?" asked Jake.

"If I didn't tell you what I told them. And I won't!"

Wally was furious. "You told them everything we were planning to do to them, didn't you? You're a snitch, Peter!"

"I am not! You said we were going to treat them like sisters, and I was just being nice."

"You told them we were going to knock down their fort, didn't you! That's why they were out there waiting to ambush us!" said Jake. "You went over there and told them!"

"I did not! I called them up."

Wally moaned. "You *are* a snitch!"

"A traitor to your brothers," said Jake.

"A weasel," said Josh.

Peter started to cry, and the boys immediately felt sorry.

"Oh, never mind," said Josh. "But the only way you can make it up to us is to call the girls and tell them you won't be giving away our plans anymore. You've either got to be in the brotherhood or you've got to go over there and live. You can't have it both ways."

"You mean I could go over and live with them?" Peter asked, brightening.

"No!" the boys all bellowed together.

"But you have to decide if you're for or against us," said Wally.

Peter thought some more.

"For," he said finally, without enthusiasm.

Wally handed him the telephone and dialed the Malloys' number.

"Hello," Peter said when someone answered. "I have to tell you I can't come over there anymore and give away secrets because I have to be a brotherhood."

Jake started to laugh. The boys waited.

For a long time, it seemed, Peter simply sat there with the telephone to his ear without saying a word.

"Who is it? What's she *saying*?" Jake asked when he couldn't wait another minute. "Boy, she must really be giving him an earful."

Peter looked at his brothers and held out the phone.

"She's crying," he said.

The boys stared at each other.

"Crying?" asked Josh. *"Who?"*

"Beth. Her mother's gone in the blizzard," Peter said.

Josh took the phone. "Beth? This is Josh. What's wrong?"

Wally sat at the table without moving. He had known the Malloy girls when they were angry, embarrassed, amused, and delighted, but he had never known one of them to cry. What were you supposed to do if a girl cried? If she was your sister?

"Yeah," Josh was saying. "Yeah. . . . Gee, I don't know. . . . Yeah, I can imagine. . . ."

And finally, to the surprise of the others, he said, "Listen, do you want us to come over?"

When he hung up, Josh said, "Their mom went to Elkins this morning, they think, and hasn't come back."

"What time did she leave?" asked Jake.

"We were trying to figure that out. Eleven, maybe. Eleven-fifteen. They tried to call their dad at the college, but he's at a meeting somewhere and they can't find him. They're scared."

Scared? What were you supposed to do when a sister was scared? Wally didn't know that either. He looked out the window and could see nothing but snow. They had a *reason* to be scared.

"Well, *that* was dumb. Who would go driving in West Virginia in a blizzard? What are *we* supposed to do about it?" said Jake.

"Maybe it wasn't snowing when she started out. No one knew there was going to be a storm like this," said Josh. He turned to Wally. "Why don't you come with me? I don't want to go over there by myself. Peter, you want to come?"

"You said I couldn't go over there again," Peter warbled.

"Just forget what we said, okay?"

"Listen, you guys, you're not going to leave me behind," said Jake. "If you're going, so am I."

So all four boys bundled up, and—holding on to each other so that they could see in the blinding snow—they crossed the road, eased themselves down the hill to the swinging bridge, and then . . . step by step . . . made their way across.

"It's a whiteout!" Jake breathed when they reached the other side. "That's what they call it in the Arctic when you can't see anything but snow."

"Can we find the way up to their house?" Peter whispered, frightened by the wind's fury.

Josh, who was in the lead, stumbled at last on a step and realized he was at the Malloys' back door. A moment later the four boys tumbled into the Malloys' kitchen.

Beth's and Caroline's eyes were red.

"We don't know whether to call the sheriff or not," Eddie said, stone-faced. "We can't reach Dad. Earlier they said he was at a meeting, and now the department answering machine comes on and says that all classes have been canceled."

The boys took off their jackets and piled them by the door.

"Are there mountains between here and Elkins?" asked Beth.

"There are some fair-sized hills," said Jake, "but she still should have been back by now if she'd wanted to beat the storm."

The phone rang and Caroline grabbed for it. It was Mrs. Hatford. The boys could hear her voice all across the kitchen.

"Caroline, I've been calling home and no one answers. I'm worried. I just heard that the schools let out early. Have you seen our boys?"

"They're over here," Caroline told her. "They came because . . . because—" And Caroline could not stop the tears. "Because our mother's m . . . missing, Mrs. Hatford. She went to Elkins this morning and we think she's lost in the blizzard." Caroline's voice ended in a sad little squeal.

"Oh, my goodness!" said Mrs. Hatford. "Have you called your father?"

"He's at a meeting. We can't find him either," Caroline wept.

"All right, here's what we'll do. I'll page my husband on his beeper, and I want all you kids to stay right where you are," Mrs. Hatford said. "Don't go out, and stay by the telephone. I'll call as soon as I get some news. Put Jake on, please."

Caroline handed the phone to Jake.

"Jake, I want all you kids to keep together now," said his mother. "Stay inside, right where you are. I'm going to find your father and tell him about Mrs. Malloy. Meanwhile, everyone in Buckman is coming to the hardware store for snow shovels and sand and flashlights and batteries, and no telling when we'll close tonight. I'll stay as long as they need me. But I want you boys to help the Malloys in any way you can."

"We will," Jake told her.

The seven sat awkwardly around the kitchen table.

"I suppose we could play a game or something while we're waiting," Wally said at last.

No one answered.

"We could always bake cookies!" Peter said brightly.

No one responded to that either.

Finally Beth got up woodenly and placed the cookie jar on the table. "Have some," she said.

Eddie put a jug of cider on the table and some plastic cups. But only Peter seemed hungry. He opened the lid. There were lemon squares and chocolate clusters, oatmeal raisin and butterscotch bars. But only Peter took a cookie. Only Peter drank some cider.

"What if she's lost in the snow?" Caroline began. "She doesn't even know the roads here in West Virginia. How long can she sit inside a car without freezing to death?"

"Oh, Caroline, shut up!" said Eddie. "Just shut up." But her own voice was shaky.

Nineteen

■

. . . And Found

The phone rang again. Eddie answered. It was Mr. Hatford.

"Eddie, I just talked to my wife. She says your mother went to Elkins today and hasn't come back. Do you know what time she left?"

"All we know is that she had an appointment at a gallery at noon. That's what it said on her calendar."

"Then I'd guess she left by eleven—maybe even before it started to snow. The only gallery I know in Elkins is the Fisher's Gallery. Is that where she went?"

"Yes."

"I just called there, but they're closed. I'm heading out that way now in my Jeep, with a plow on the front. I'll take the road she would have traveled and see what I can find out. It's bound to be slow going, but I've got my cell phone. As soon as I know anything, I'll call. In the meantime, you kids sit tight."

"Okay. And thank you," Eddie said. She hung up

and turned to the Hatfords. "Your dad's going to look for her in his Jeep."

"What if *he* gets stuck in the snow?" asked Peter. Now it looked as though *he* might cry. He'd started to eat another cookie but put it back down on the table.

"Let's play Monopoly," Beth suggested, trying to hide her worry.

"I'll make popcorn," said Eddie without enthusiasm.

"I could make hot chocolate," said Caroline.

Everyone seemed grateful for the distraction. Beth set up the board at the kitchen table, Eddie made the popcorn, and Caroline got down the mugs for cocoa. Soon they were choosing pieces, drawing cards, passing Go, and buying properties. But their eyes traveled frequently to the window, their ears listening for the phone. When it rang at last around four, they all jumped. Once again Caroline answered.

"Caroline, I've just come from a meeting and heard that everything is closing early today. Things okay there?" asked her father.

"No!" Caroline said. "Mom's missing!" And suddenly she began to sob.

"What?"

Beth got on the phone next and explained what had happened, how the Hatford boys had come over to keep them company, and that their dad was heading for Elkins in his Jeep.

"I'll be home as soon as I can get a ride with someone in a four-wheel drive," her father said. "My car's completely snowed under."

The seven began playing Monopoly again, but

when an hour had gone by and still there was no call, no Mr. Malloy, the Monopoly game stopped. No one felt like playing anymore. Half the popcorn went uneaten. Half the cocoa was left in the cups.

Then the lights went out. The refrigerator stopped humming. There would be no TV. No radio.

"We will all die," said Caroline softly.

"Caroline, shut *up*!" Beth scolded.

"Is the phone still working?" Eddie asked.

Beth checked. It was. She called the weather bureau. There was a travelers' advisory. The storm was letting up, it said, but people were advised to stay inside, not to drive unless they had to. Road conditions were treacherous. There had been accidents. . . .

The house grew colder. Eddie and Beth went upstairs and returned with armfuls of blankets. Each of the seven wrapped up in a blanket, and they all hunkered down on the floor beside the living room window, waiting for the blizzard to pass. Another hour went by. Six o'clock. Six-thirty. . . .

"Now *Dad's* missing," Caroline gulped.

"Oh, he'll be all right," Eddie said. "It's Mom I'm—" She didn't finish.

"Well, our dad's been out in lots of storms," said Wally finally. "He's a pretty good driver. He'll find her." But he didn't sound at all sure.

"Yeah," said Jake. "If anyone can find your mom, it's Dad. He's got all sorts of stuff in his Jeep—two-way radio, cell phone, beeper, first-aid kit, ax . . ."

"Ax?" squeaked Caroline.

- - -

"In case he has to chop someone out of a wrecked car," said Peter.

"Be quiet, Peter," murmured Jake. And then to the girls, "If Dad didn't think he could find her, he wouldn't have gone out."

And Josh added, "We won't leave here until he does, okay?"

Beth looked over at him. "I'm glad you guys are here," she said in a small voice.

"So are we," Josh told her.

But Caroline sat leaning against the wall in her blanket, nothing showing except her eyes. "This is the way they will find us," she said in a pitiful voice. "Seven icicles wrapped in blankets. Seven frozen bodies, too cold and weak to move. Seven people who might have become famous when they were grown, but—"

And then the lights came on. Everyone cheered, even Caroline, who had had her sad story cut short. The furnace clicked on, and so did the refrigerator.

"Ya-hoo!" yelled Peter, throwing off his blanket and hopping around.

The phone rang, and this time Eddie answered.

"I found your mom," came Mr. Hatford's voice. "Her car went off the road into a ditch, but she's fine. We're on our way. Don't know what time we'll get there, but I've got a Thermos of coffee with us, and we'll be all right."

"Hooray!" everyone yelled when they heard the news. Caroline didn't think she had ever felt more relieved or happy. She reached for the closest person to hug, discovered it was Wally, then dived down in her blanket again.

There was the sound of a truck pulling into the Malloys' driveway. The girls ran to the door and turned on the porch light, then swarmed around their father as he came inside, waving a thank-you to the driver of a pickup.

"Mom's okay! Mr. Hatford found her, and they're on their way home!" Caroline told him, hugging him hard.

Mr. Malloy's face sagged with relief. "Well, that's the best news I've had all day. You must have thought I was lost too. I waited an hour but couldn't find a ride home, so I set out on foot, and it was one adventure after another. People were stuck all over the place. Finally a pickup truck offered me a ride, and darned if *we* didn't get stuck."

He stomped his feet and took off his coat.

"Hi, guys," he said to the Hatfords. "I hear your dad's a hero."

Wally grinned. "He's used to stuff like this. Mail carriers have to go out in all kinds of weather."

"Well, I'm mighty grateful to him. It's going to take some time for the weather bureau to live *this* storm down. What was supposed to be light snow turned out to be a full-fledged blizzard and no one was prepared." He looked around the kitchen. "Why don't you fellas stay till your folks get home? We'll hustle up something for dinner."

"No, we'll be fine," said Jake. "Maybe we'll go home and make dinner for Mom."

"Be sure to make her some brownies!" Caroline said mischievously.

The girls chattered on about what had happened that day, but when they stopped for breath, they realized that the boys had put on their coats and were getting ready to leave. Somehow everything seemed different now, Caroline thought. The light was so bright, the kitchen so cheery, the boys so . . . so *fat*! Strangely fat and cheerful! They looked like overstuffed furniture, in fact.

"Thanks for coming over," Beth said as she opened the door for them. "I mean it."

And from behind her, Caroline squeaked, "With you by my side, Elmer, we can do anything!"

Everyone grinned, and Wally added, "Annabelle, I never thought I'd amount to much, but when I met you, everything changed!"

"Cut it out," said Josh, turning red, but he was smiling too.

"I'm outta here," said Jake, and his brothers followed him out the door.

The girls went back inside, laughing. For the first time since they'd gotten home that day they actually *felt* like laughing. For the first time that afternoon they were actually hungry.

"Let's heat up the cocoa again," said Caroline.

"Cocoa and cookies," said Beth. She lifted the lid on the cookie jar.

It was empty—totally empty. No lemon squares, no chocolate clusters, no oatmeal raisin, no butterscotch bars. Not one cookie. Not even a crumb.

"Nothing!" said Eddie.

"But hardly anyone was eating!" said Caroline. "No one was hungry!"

"Three dozen cookies! Gone!" cried Beth.

"As soon as those guys found out everyone was safe, they started stuffing themselves!" said Eddie. "All the time we were talking to Dad, they were squirreling away cookies in every pocket they own! They were stuffing cookies up their sleeves, I'll bet!"

"That's boys for you," said Mr. Malloy from the next room.

"This means war!" said Caroline.

"Ha! It never stopped!" said Eddie, her eyes full of excitement. "Just wait till they see what's coming next!"

The Boys Start the War

Just when the Hatford brothers were expecting three boys to move into the house across the river, where their best friends used to live, the Malloy girls arrive instead. Wally and his brothers decide to make Caroline and her sisters so miserable that they'll want to go back to Ohio, but they haven't counted on the ingenuity of the girls. From dead fish to dead bodies, floating cakes to floating heads, the pranks and tricks continue—first by the boys, then by the girls—until someone is taken prisoner!

The Girls Get Even

Still smarting over the boys' latest trick on them, the girls are determined to get even. Caroline's thrilled to play the part of Goblin Queen in the school play, especially since Wally Hatford has to be her footman. The boys, however, have a creepy plan for Halloween night. They are certain the girls will walk right into their trap. Little do the boys know what the Malloy sisters have in store.

Boys Against Girls

Abaguchie mania! Caroline Malloy shivers happily when her on-again, off-again enemy Wally Hatford tells her that a strange animal known as the abaguchie has been spotted in their area. According to Wally, an abaguchie skeleton was found years ago in the cellar of Oldakers' Bookstore. Wally swears Caroline to secrecy and warns her not to search for herself. But Caroline will do anything to find the secret of the bones.

A Spy Among the Girls

Valentine's Day is coming up, and love is in the air for Beth Malloy and Josh Hatford. When they're spotted holding hands, Josh tells his teasing brothers that he's simply spying on the girls to see what they're plotting next. At the same time, Caroline Malloy, the family actress, decides she must know what it's like to fall in love. Poor Wally Hatford is in for it when she chooses him as the object of her affection!

The Boys Return

It's spring break, and the only assignment Wally Hatford and Caroline Malloy have is to do something they've never done before. Wally's sure that will be a cinch, because the mighty Benson brothers are coming. It will be nonstop action all the way. For starters, the nine Benson and Hatford boys plan to scare the three Malloy sisters silly by convincing them that their house is haunted. Meanwhile, everyone in town has heard that there's a hungry cougar on the prowl. When the kids decide to take a break from their tricks and join forces to catch the cougar, guess who gets stuck with the scariest job?

About the Author

Phyllis Reynolds Naylor enjoys writing about the Hatford boys and the Malloy girls because the books take place in her husband's home state, West Virginia. The town of Buckman in the stories is really Buckhannon, where her husband spent most of his growing-up years. Mrs. Naylor plans to write one book for each month that the girls are in Buckman, though who knows whether or not they will move back to Ohio at the end?

Phyllis Reynolds Naylor is the author of more than a hundred books, a number of which are set in West Virginia, including the Newbery Award–winning *Shiloh* and the other two books in the Shiloh triology, *Shiloh Season* and *Saving Shiloh*. She and her husband live in Bethesda, Maryland.